ADON CADDO at the BLACK GARDENIA

GARY STEPHEN MOORE

WestBow
PRESS®
A DIVISION OF THOMAS NELSON
& ZONDERVAN

Copyright © 2017 Gary Stephen Moore.

All rights reserved. No part of this book may be used or reproduced by any means, graphic, electronic, or mechanical, including photocopying, recording, taping or by any information storage retrieval system without the written permission of the author except in the case of brief quotations embodied in critical articles and reviews.

This is a work of fiction. All of the characters, names, incidents, organizations, and dialogue in this novel are either the products of the author's imagination or are used fictitiously.

WestBow Press books may be ordered through booksellers or by contacting:

WestBow Press
A Division of Thomas Nelson & Zondervan
1663 Liberty Drive
Bloomington, IN 47403
www.westbowpress.com
1 (866) 928-1240

Because of the dynamic nature of the Internet, any web addresses or links contained in this book may have changed since publication and may no longer be valid. The views expressed in this work are solely those of the author and do not necessarily reflect the views of the publisher, and the publisher hereby disclaims any responsibility for them.

Any people depicted in stock imagery provided by Thinkstock are models, and such images are being used for illustrative purposes only. Certain stock imagery © Thinkstock.

Scripture quotes are taken from the King James Version of the Bible.

ISBN: 978-1-5127-7160-2 (sc)
ISBN: 978-1-5127-7162-6 (hc)
ISBN: 978-1-5127-7161-9 (e)

Library of Congress Control Number: 2017900282

Print information available on the last page.

WestBow Press rev. date: 2/2/2017

For my wonderful, outrageous family
from whom I have learned so much!

For thereby some have entertained angels unawares.
—Hebrews 13:2 (King James Version)

PROLOGUE

It stood there, beyond legend. No one knew when it was built, by whom, how, or even why, for that matter. It was just there — a dilapidated shack totally out of sorts with the huts of the surrounding native inhabitants. It was overgrown with aromatic jasmine, moon vine, ivy, and other exotic vines that defied horticultural description. Anything that went to seed in its vicinity grew, most beyond the norm for their species or genus.

On the outside, it was shielded from the light of day by massive, ancient, moss-laden oaks made red by their proximity to the water, a mystery unto itself. Their size made it extremely difficult for sunlight to penetrate (though the light of a full moon never had a problem and always seemed to infiltrate the dense canopy). Weathered and distressed shutters that had certainly witnessed their share of violent tempests shielded the inside.

It had one visible entrance: an ancient, weathered door that lacked knob and hinges. It was reached via a wood-planked pier, supported by rickety wooden poles that skimmed the surface of the swamp's reddish water. Vegetation grew thick upon the water's surface, most notably wild water lilies and pungent swamp lotus.

On those nights that were not blessed by a full moon, illumination was provided by millions of zealous lightning bugs that somehow knew it was their sacred duty to light the walkway. If they did not, the chance visitor might never be assured of finding the hidden entrance.

The shack was surrounded by a nearly impenetrable flowering

hedge of glistening, black, aromatic blossoms that towered over the roofline. The fragrance that exuded from these blossoms could cause one to lose the ability to retain the deep, dark secrets hidden within the farthest reaches of one's soul.

The most peculiar feature of the shack, however, was that it was larger on the inside than on the outside. Many individuals would discover this unique feature over the ages, as they were influenced by the power, and the wonder, of the Black Gardenia, as it was known for as long as anyone could remember.

The structure bore no trace of nail, peg, glue, or any other means that bound its multiple parts together. The only bonding agent, if you could call it that, was a kind of incandescent red light. As a result, its slats and beams were able to breathe with the atmospheric variations.

Was it forbidding? Perhaps to those unprepared to delve into explorations that plummeted the depths of their psyches.

Even though the Black Gardenia rested among the lush foliage of the swamp, it did so in a silence quite profound. Even the cacophony produced by the native wildlife was reverently hushed in its presence. It should be noted, though, that once in a while, the shriek of a common loon would pierce the pungent atmosphere. That sound announced the emergence of an individual from the Black Gardenia, though the emergence was rarely back to their original time and location.

As forbidding as the Black Gardenia could be, it was a place that called to individuals, regardless of their status or location in life. It harbored no biased agenda, nor did it segregate individual from individual or species from species. It was an equal-opportunity domain. And it was alive! Even more peculiar, at times a blood-red light glowed from deep within, transforming the swamp into something quite extraordinary. Why, or how, no one dared venture a guess. It just did.

CHAPTER 1
ADON CADDO

Caddo is a word that is frequently heard in the American Deep South. Loosely translated, it means "red river" or "red waters." Current etymological belief states that it was a Native American term, perhaps influenced by the French word *caddeaux*. It was not. Furthermore, it was not native to the South. Nor did it originate on the North American landmass, this world, or for that matter, this universe. In truth, its origin (how best to say it?) was derived from the heavenly tongue. In other words, Caddo is of divine origins.

In the time before time, the Great One created the Adons (or "Lords"). Their purpose was to act as overlords in part of the Great One's vast, eternal plan (i.e., the division and continuation of His chosen humans into a priesthood and twelve distinct tribes in preparation of His advent on this terrestrial sphere).

Though the Adons were of the angelic order, they were scarcely visible to any mortal eye, if at all. They rarely altered the course of human events. However, they could influence events through subtle acts of persuasion: a whisper here, a suggestion there.

Each of the Adons was associated with a specific precious stone that corresponded to one of the twelve tribes that corresponded to the twelve gates of the heavenly kingdom. Because of the Adons, one of the Great One's appellations was Adonai (the plural of Adon).

Highest ranked among the Adons was Adon Caddo. He glowed as red as a ruby and was entrusted to oversee those who had been designated as high priests of the Great One.

CHAPTER 2

THE CHOSEN

Very early, as the Great One's process unfolded, a particular individual had caught the attention of Adon Caddo. Then it happened—an event of astounding importance: A forlorn, little brushwood bush caught fire on the side of a desolate, high mountain.

One day, the particular individual whom Adon Caddo had been entrusted to observe, encourage, and influence, if necessary, was awakened from a very disturbed, deep slumber by that voice, *again*. He knew that voice. For years, it had plotted out the course of his turbulent and tempestuous life.

Adon Caddo could never understand this chosen man. Though certainly charismatic, he was quite scruffy and very irritable. In his youth, he had been a princely figure of an exotic kingdom. He had slept upon the finest linens, but now his bed was the hard earth, with only a roughly woven blanket for warmth. He once smelled of the finest perfumes; now he smelled of livestock and dung. He had been raised on endless varieties of succulent foods, but now he was reduced to humble meals of bread and quail.

Adon Caddo could never comprehend the needs of such an earthly, physical creature. He had no need of sustenance because he was continuously, and directly, nourished by the Great One Himself.

After his assignment, Adon Caddo accompanied this chosen one on every path the Great One had laid out for him. It was, however, always an issue for the Great One to get the chosen's attention. It wasn't complacency; the chosen one had seen the Great One's handiwork far too many times. No, it was irritation. He was actually irritated that the Great One still had something up His sleeve that was guaranteed, he was convinced, to cause him tremendous grief and hardship. He had discovered over the years, however, that the only way to get the Great One off his back was to comply.

The chosen's exotic countrymen had long ceased their worship of him because of his exile and banishment. Those he now led followed him because they had no one else and nowhere else to go. They did not genuflect when he would emerge from his tent or walk through their midst. Rather, they grumbled, moaned, and groaned at even the thought of his arrival. They never grasped the wonder and significance that occurred on their behalf through this chosen one's begrudging willingness to be the pliant tool of the Great One.

Adon Caddo couldn't believe that this particular individual would have the cheek to actually be irritated, but irritated he was because he had been roused from his slumber. As the chosen one finally decided to follow his instinct, he sluggishly walked up the mountain. And then suddenly, something caught his eye. In the middle of nowhere on the side of this barren mountain, he saw a flaming bush. He stared at it for what seemed hours, but the bush was never consumed. Then the Great One's voice spoke out of the flame directly to him, causing him to prostrate himself upon the ground.

It never ceased to amuse Adon Caddo to see this arrogant individual respond as His voice permeated and spoke to every molecule of his body. Adon Caddo was overwhelmed and overcome. He trembled and covered his face as the voice spoke.

Since time was irrelevant to an eternal being, Adon Caddo had no reason to understand the length of time the chosen one had remained sprawled face down on the ground, nor how long it took the Great One to bestow upon him the stone tablets of His governance. All Adon Caddo was aware of was the chosen's descent down the mountain, vibrantly aglow with the light of the Divine. Now the great congregation of the chosen's countrymen took notice and bowed low before him (though it was really the light of the Divine they actually acknowledged).

From this point, the existence of Adon Caddo, as well as the other Adons, took on a more significant, and unusual, direction.

CHAPTER 3
THE VEIL AND BEYOND

Adon Caddo was there when the Great One had His people construct an Ark designed specifically to be the seat of His presence. He wandered unseen in that forsaken desert for all those years, as they carried the Ark from place to place. He was there when the waters of the Jordan River were parted, and he was most excited when the priests carried the ark around Jericho, and the walls of that evil city of the moon crashed to the ground. He stood with the chosen one when he was not permitted entrance into the Promised Land, and he bitterly lamented when the chosen one was no more.

This was the first, but certainly not the last, time that Adon Caddo felt a sense of disorientation and loss. He knew, however, that his function was not to serve the created but to serve the Creator, regardless of the circumstances. So he girded his metaphorical loins, gritted his teeth, and pressed on, regardless of where the Great One led him.

His journeys continued as he followed the triumph and tragedy of these chosen people. Adon Caddo was horrified when the Ark was captured, and he was there when the Glory departed. He rejoiced when the Glory returned and rejoiced even more when the great king brought it to the city of peace. Adon Caddo was ecstatic when the Ark found a permanent resting place inside the wonders of the great new temple and when the glory of the Great One descended.

He traveled to that wicked country when the city of peace had been destroyed and all had been taken captive. He and the other Adons were dismayed and had no idea if the Ark had come with them. It had simply vanished.

Adon Caddo followed the priesthood upon their release from captivity, and he was there when the prophet foresaw the advent of the great High King Priest, the One. He stood and sang with the other Adons as the angelic chorus burst through time when the One was born.

Adon Caddo frequently got the opportunity, as did the other Adons, to trouble the waters at the Pool of Bethesda. It delighted him to see the blind, halt, and withered people receive a healing.

Of most significance, Adon Caddo was there on that horrible day when the veil was rent in two, and he was horrified as the temple was torn asunder and the priesthood destroyed. All of the Adons simply stared, unable to fathom what had taken place. And then, in the twinkling of a second, stunned, grief stricken, and dismayed, they were back in their celestial home, as the great High King Priest spoke four words to the depths of their being:

"Wait, Watch, Work, Witness."

These words were followed by one command, and one command only: The Adons were to never leave their new homes until the Great One summoned them from heaven. The Adons had never been presented with such a situation before; none felt it to be an odd or some impossible request. It just was.

As suddenly as the Adons had been brought home, they were flung back into the creation; each landed in a different location on that blue orb, each at the mouth of a different great river, where each waterway served as the main artery for each location.

For the first time, the Adons were separated by time and space. For the first time since their creation, they were without each other, alone. It took quite a while for the disorientation to wear off. When it did, they discovered that it was now up to each of them independently to discover for themselves how they were to utilize their unique gifts. This was, after all, a part of His great plan.

Adon Caddo found that he was now in a sweltering and humid land of swampy waterways, overgrown with all forms of vegetation. He knew that He who measured the waters in the hollow of His hand, measured heaven with a span, calculated the dust of the earth in a measure, and weighed the mountains in scales and the hills in a balance, also knew perfectly well where Adon Caddo was. So, rather than be discontent in his new surrounding, he obediently chose to make the best of it.

Adon Caddo needed a form of seclusion but something still accessible to those whom he might welcome and help. After a while, he found the perfect spot: a tiny island in the midst of a swamp where grew a spectacular variety of land-born and water-born flowers, majestic moss-laden trees, and a plethora of plants. Most unique were the towering hedges of glistening black, fragrant blossoms that he saw nowhere else and which gave the appearance and impression of guardians.

As he came closer to the island, he felt his powers return, and he was actually invigorated. Adon Caddo realized that, for now, he was home.

A piece of driftwood floated by and caught his eye. He pointed his finger at it, and with his summons, it rose from the water and drifted through the air toward a central position on the island. He repeated this over and over with every piece of driftwood he discovered. Without the use of nail or peg, the driftwoods assembled into the semblance of a shack. With the remainder, he constructed a walkway from the shore to his island.

When night began to fall, Adon Caddo walked across the planks to his new home. He was accompanied by millions of lightning bugs that lit his way. They were to remain with him for the duration of his new assignment at his home, the Black Gardenia.

As his passion for the life the Great One had given him swelled within his heart, he sat down and contentedly ran his fingers through the murky green water. Upon his touch, the water began to glow red. Little currents carried the water out of the realm of his home and, over time, transformed the adjoining waterways.

The next morning, his attention was diverted to a strange cawing/gurgling racket. When he went outside, there before him stood a large white bird with an extremely wide wingspan, a giant beak, and a huge filmy sack under its beak. Adon Caddo had never seen such a peculiar winged creature as that which stood before him. The bird, with quite a self-assured attitude, walked up to Adon Caddo and stared straight into his eyes. Adon Caddo knew immediately that the bird's proper name was Pelicandray, but he answered to "Pel," if he so desired.

After that first encounter, Pel was his constant companion and remained around that little island of the Black Gardenia. Pel considered himself to be Adon Caddo's wing man. A special bond formed between them; Pel followed Adon Caddo everywhere.

CHAPTER 4

HOME

Throughout the swamps, there lived an aboriginal people whose origins were shrouded in mystery. Most believed that thousands of years earlier, they had migrated from where the golden sun rose from its slumber. When they did finally settle in and around the swamps, they defined their boundaries by four sacred trees that grew at each of the cardinal points. They believed that these four trees were imbued with divine powers and, therefore, worthy of worship.

They relied on the swamp for both sustenance and protection. They even used it for recreation, but always with a cautious eye. It did not take them long to realize that something most strange had begun on what they had always believed was an insignificant little island. Word spread through the swamps that great magic had arrived. This, of course, could shatter their eon-old system of belief. They realized that great caution, with a large dose of immense wonder, was in order.

What most disturbed (but fascinated) them was that, from their continuous contact with the water, their skin had gradually turned from a tanned yellow to a lustrous deep red. At first horrified, they began to wonder at and then admire their transformation. They assumed the name the People Altogether Red.

Adon Caddo had been able to stay out of their sight for years, but he knew it was only a matter of time before he was discovered. He began to notice little offerings of flowers as they appeared on the shore side of the walkway, but he thought little of it. He was alarmed when offerings of food were left, but he was horrified when a tiny child, starved and beaten, was abandoned at the walkway.

Adon Caddo took the child into the interior expanse of the Black Gardenia and whispered to it, "Those who live in the hidden places of the Great One will do so in the shadow of His presence. Nothing, little one, shall ever harm you again."

The red glow of Adon Caddo then engulfed the child and brought sudden and complete healing. The child stood in full strength and purpose. As the song of the common loon sang out, the child emerged from the Black Gardenia, never again to be recognized by the miscreants who had abandoned it. The child walked into the arms of a new family, who cherished the gift they had been given.

Adon Caddo was stunned and strangely affected by this. Something moved him deeply as he realized he now had the power to interact rather than to observe. Perhaps, he thought, this was the beginning of his new work. Only time would tell.

Until now, the people were afraid of the island. Adon Caddo realized that if they discovered him, he would be worshipped as a deity. This was something he could never permit. So late one night, he began to sing. In the light of the full moon, millions of fireflies responded to his voice and began a luminous gavotte. As Adon Caddo stood under the towering Black Gardenias, the fireflies intricately wove a hooded cassock out of vines, leaves, flowers, and light. When it was complete, Adon Caddo blended into the environment so completely that no one would have guessed that he was even there.

He then realized that the fireflies were willing to assist with any task he had for them. Adon Caddo began to practice under the canopy of darkness: He would thrust an arm out from under his new cassock, and a line of fireflies immediately responded by forming a shimmering line from his fingertips in the direction he pointed. If he curled his fingers, the fireflies would make a loop of light. If he spread his fingers, the fireflies would create five luminous lines. Adon Caddo was enchanted by this new development and continued to practice until the sun rose.

To the delight of Adon Caddo, the mystique of the Black Gardenia never diminished. In fact, it only grew with the passing of time.

Adon Caddo found contentment on his little island in the middle of the swamp, in the middle of nowhere. The locals, well aware that something utterly strange was in residence on that island, maintained their wary distance. Adon Caddo was able to help them discreetly, without drawing attention to himself. Their proximity to the Black Gardenia ensured that their bounty would increase beyond measure, when compared to neighboring tribes. For the most part, however, regardless of the hints and suggestions he might leave to spurn their innate curiosity to seek out the Great One he so loved, Adon Caddo was unable to alter their allegiance from their tribal deities. Their hearts were fixed, and as a result, their largess was to drastically change.

CHAPTER 5
MAMA BAYOU

Though not an orphan, Martine might as well have been: The youngest of eight siblings, she was nothing more than chattel, a scullery maid in the small country inn her parents ran far outside the parameters of Paris. Her life was a monotonous, grueling misery, with her only comfort being long walks along the banks of the stream when she could sneak away. It was on one of these walks when she heard Him.

Martine first heard the voice of the Great One when she was very small. It was a warm spring day, and as she walked along a stream, she heard Him say quite clearly, "Whatever you do for the least of my brethren, you do for me."[1] She was not blinded by a vision, the world did not come to a halt, nor did she go into babbling fits of religious ecstasy with vocal spasms of glossolalia. She simply knew that she must follow His voice to wherever it led.

When she returned home, her father, furious with her for being late, struck her so hard she practically flew across the common room. The usual malefactors, outcasts, and reprobates who frequented the inn took little notice.

As she wept, Martine ran outside, directly into three young nuns who were passing by. One of the young women took Martine's face in her hands, wiped off her tear-stained face, and asked, "Child, are you all right?"

No one had ever expressed any interest in or concern for her before. Martine was thoroughly beguiled.

"Oh please, miss," said Martine, "take me with you! Help me get away from here. I'll do anything you ask."

"Dear child, as much as we would like to help you, we simply cannot. In a few days, our order will leave France for the New World. That's no place for a child, and besides, we could not take you from your parents."

"They wouldn't even notice that I'm gone; they wouldn't!" pleaded Martine. "Please take me with you."

"Now, child, run along before you get into further trouble. May God bless and keep you."

The sisters continued on their walk. Martine, however, did not do as they asked but chose to follow them instead.

"What was worse," she pondered, "to remain here where my life was threatened daily, or go to somewhere new, somewhere I'm not known?"

With great stealth, Martine followed the sisters (who had now been joined by eleven others), and after many hours, they arrived at the port where their ship, the *Gironde*, was in final preparations for the voyage. It was a simple matter for Martine to slip on board under cover of night and to hide herself amongst the various crates and other things being shipped. She then fell asleep and was totally unaware when the ship left port. She awoke to the sound of the sisters, who sang praise and thanksgiving to God. As sweet as their song was, Martine realized that she could not live on their songs alone; she must find food if she was to make it to the New World.

Her hiding place was dry and secure; she could hide out with relative security. Every night, once the crew and passengers had retired, Martine would quietly sneak out of her hiding place and hunt for any food she might be lucky enough to find. It was on one of these excursions that she met the mother superior, Sister Saint Augustin, who was unable to sleep. She had decided to walk about the deck and gaze at the vast canopy of stars overhead. Suddenly,

Sister Saint Augustin caught movement out of the corner of her eyes and, upon careful scrutiny, realized that it was the little girl she had encountered at that country inn. Sister Saint Augustin followed the scavenging movements of the child and realized that she must help this poor wretch, but she did not want to get her in any trouble with the captain. So every evening, Sister Saint Augustin made sure that she saved a portion of her meal, and as she strolled about on the deck for her evening prayers, she would find little places where food could be hidden, with the hope that the child would not starve.

It was only a matter of time, however, before Martine was found out. This happened when the *Gironde* encountered a storm. As all deckhands scrambled about to secure the cargo, Martine was thrust from her place of hiding. In the wind, rain, and commotion, she was mistaken as one of the lackeys and so went undetected by the ship's crew. Sister Saint Augustin, however, noticed Martine's attempt to remain hidden, an eventual impossibility. She suddenly rushed to Martine, engulfed her within the folds of her habit, and took her back to her room, where she announced, "Look, we have a guest!"

She thrust Martine from the folds of her habit into the center of their tiny room. The other sisters gasped and then all huddled about their new ward, as they dried her off and continued to ride out the tempest.

The following morning, the sisters realized that they had a very real problem on their hands. If they told the captain of Martine's illegal presence, there was no telling what he would do. As they prayed for guidance, Martine suddenly offered a suggestion: Perhaps she could join their order. The sisters were at first stunned. Quickly, however, they beamed as the light of epiphany began to shine. As a postulant, Martine could be trained and yet still have the choice, and chance, of changing her mind if she discovered that this was not what she ultimately desired for her life.

The sisters were able to fashion a habit for Martine out of their own belongings. They agreed that they would never leave her alone but would always stay together in groups of three or four. The captain and crew looked upon them as intrusions, anyway, so they were basically ignored.

Every morning, the sisters would have morning prayers and worship on deck, where they could enjoy and praise the vastness of God's creation. During the day, they would tend to the business of Martine's education or attempt to enlighten the crew (which many felt to be a pointless endeavor; their hope was that one never knew what would happen after a spiritual seed was planted). In this fashion, the Ursulines passed their remaining time on the voyage.

When at last the Port of New Orleans had been sighted, the sisters gathered on deck and sang songs of praise; even the crew joined in the celebration. After the long voyage, the miracle was not only that they had arrived safe and sound, but also Martine had never been discovered. And so, as the sisters disembarked from the *Gironde*, the captain stood by the gangplank that led to the dock and scratched his head, most confused. He could not figure out how the fourteen sisters had become fifteen. It was too late to do anything about it, so he just ignored it and went on about his business. New Orleans now had not fourteen but fifteen new residents to add to the ever-increasing mix of nationalities.

The moment Martine set foot in New Orleans, she was galvanized by the bustling mix of nationalities, the pungent aromas, the heat, the humidity, the light, and the profuse vegetation that all mingled into one overwhelming sensation that got under her skin and transformed her. She was home.

The sisters first went to a large house that had been secured for them by the king. They immediately established a convent and school, where they began their mission: to provide a practical, artistic, and spiritual education for young women and girls of all nationalities and status. It took little time before news of their success returned to France. This prompted even more sisters to make the voyage and join this exciting work in New Orleans.

The success of the Ursulines' work kept Sister Martine (as she was now called) exceptionally busy. When not at work, Sister Martine's curiosity would provoke her to take long walks around the city. When she felt very adventuresome, she would venture along the mysterious bayous. These walks soon became a passion for her: The secrets of the bayous were of endless fascination to her. She rarely encountered anyone, but when she did, a simple nod of the head was all that was required to acknowledge each other's presence.

On one of her walks, she noticed that the water of the bayou had started to take on a reddish cast. This intrigued her, and she decided to find out why. As she walked along the bayou, a white pelican suddenly appeared in her path, startling her. It just stood there and stared at her. It then turned away, glanced back as if to entice her to follow, and waddled toward a wooden pier, where it sat down. Martine followed, and when she got next to the pelican, she sat down beside it, removed her shoes, and let her feet dangle in the surprisingly cool red water.

Martine surveyed her surroundings and noticed a tiny island on which stood a dilapidated shack. Curiosity got the best of her; she got up to examine the shack, but the pelican walked quickly to block her path. Martine sat down, and the pelican sat down. She stood up, and the pelican stood up. This most bizarre bird perplexed and intrigued her.

The day had gotten late, and Martine knew she needed to return to the convent. When she turned to go, the pelican squawked, as if to say good-bye. She walked several yards and then turned around to see if the pelican had followed her. It had not, but there was a very unusual shrub, loaded with vines and blossoms, that she had not noticed before, now in sight on the island.

Back at the convent, as the number of students increased, Sister Martine's work increased. She always found a time, however, when she could go on her long walk that always ended up by the little pier that stretched to that mysterious little island, surrounded by the red waters.

It soon became a ritual: Whenever Sister Martine would show up at the pier, the pelican would suddenly appear, waddle toward her, and sit down by her side. She would talk to the bird as if it was her closest confidant, and it would look at her as if it knew precisely what she meant. When she would leave, she would always turn around, and that peculiar shrub would once again be visible at the other end of the pier.

Weeks turned into months, and months into years, but Sister Martine never missed her walks. She became such a regular feature on the dirt road that ran alongside the bayou that people began to call her Sister Bayou. Then, as she grew older, she became known as Mama Bayou.

Something else had begun to happen that quite dismayed Sister Martine, and all the other sisters as well. They noticed that her feet had begun to turn red. This she attributed to the red water surrounding that strange little island. In the convent, it was impossible to keep such a secret, so the curiosity of the sisters caused them to plead with Sister Martine to take them to that magical spot she loved so much. Try as she might, though, whenever she took a companion on her walk, she could never find her way back to that special place. Eventually, the sisters, who had begun to think that it was all delusion, gave up and allowed Sister Martine her idiosyncratic privacy. Not surprisingly, however, every time she went alone, she was able to return to the shore across from that little island, where she would be greeted by the pelican (which never seemed to age) and would notice that the shrub was in a different location. Further, every time she would sit and let her feet dangle in the red waters, the pelican would bring her a most unusual blossom; it was luxuriously black, with an intoxicating aroma. As she would return to the convent, she would inhale the aroma of the blossom, but once inside the city limits, it would wither in her hand and turn to ash.

Over the years, Sister Martine had grown from an awkward little child into full maturity. What was most unusual, and what became a source of gossip, was that she never seemed to show signs of age, much to the secret envy of those sisters who had come from France with her, who by now were getting on in years.

She was beloved by all the sisters and was a favorite of those she helped. No one ever questioned her devotion to Him whom she served or those she helped. Though completely unaware of it, she had become what His voice had said to her those many years ago.

The advent of the Europeans had brought strange new diseases, which struck the indigenous populations with a vengeance. Whenever illness would afflict a native village, Sister Martine, or Mama Bayou, as she was now addressed openly, would be there to help. She would first go to the pier, and with each visit, she would move incrementally closer to the island, with the hope of discovering its secrets. And always, as she dangled her feet in the water and prayed for guidance, Sister Martine would be greeted by that ageless pelican that would come sit by her side, black blossom in beak.

On one of her outings after she had left the pier, blossom in hand, she heard many frantic little voices call out to her, "Mama Bayou, Mama Bayou!" Suddenly, several native children grabbed her by the hands and quickly pulled her along. They led her into their village where, surrounded by many elders, she was led into a poorly lit hut that reeked of disease. There before her lay several natives, adult and children alike. All bore the same symptoms: vomiting, diarrhea, sunken eyes, cold to the touch, and wrinkling skin. Though no doctor, by this time, Sister Martine had become aware of the symptoms of cholera.

She noticed that the blossom had not turned to ash. Instinctively, she rubbed it between her palms and then went from person to person, where she laid hands on them and blessed them as she prayed for their recovery.

Days turned into weeks as Sister Martine remained with the natives until, one miraculous morning, each of the afflicted rose from their pallets, completely healed. She knew her work had reached completion and so decided that the time had come to return to the convent.

Unknown to Sister Martine, however, things had taken a surprising turn back at the convent. News of the revolution and the Reign of Terror that had broken out in France had reached the ears of the Mother Superior, who became terrified that the same horrors France experienced would soon become a reality in New Orleans. So rather than ride out an imagined storm, she impetuously, and quite arrogantly, petitioned the governor of Cuba for refuge in Havana, which he quickly granted. The sisters waited as long as they could for Sister Martine to return, but they decided they could wait no longer. They rapidly packed up their belongings and boarded a ship bound for Cuba.

After Sister Martine felt her wards were healthy, she left the village and made the long walk back to New Orleans. As she left the village, the inhabitants lined the pathway and reverently bowed as she passed.

When she finally returned to the convent, Martine was stunned to find it vacant. Frantic to discover what had happened, she ran from house to house to discover the reason. When the truth was finally known, it left her hurt and utterly distraught: Those whom she most loved and trusted had abandoned her. Devastated and confused, Martine wandered the streets of New Orleans to well past midnight. Under the light of the full moon, Martine reached the outskirts of town, where she continued out of habit on that old familiar path that she had trod so many times before.

As she neared the pier, a line of fireflies flew toward her, encircled her, and gently led her across the water and to the island, where the pelican waited for her. It waddled toward her and sat down; she then sat down beside this most peculiar bird.

Martine heard a rustling sound behind her. Without turning to see what it was, she simply said, "I know that you are there. Please show yourself."

A voice like deep music spoke, saying, "That I cannot do."

"Then please tell me who you are."

"I am the Adon Caddo."

"Whom do you serve?" Martine further inquired.

"I serve Him who was, and is, and is to come, the alpha and the omega, the beginning and the end."[2]

"What am I to do?" she inquired of the voice.

"Your greatest work is yet before you," said the voice. "You have developed the tools he destined you to possess: compassion, dedication, faith, and a trusting heart. With these, you will move mountains and be able to face the trials that will soon confront you."

"But," Martine began to protest, "who am I to be so entrusted?"

"You are His beloved, with whom He is well pleased. He knows your trust and faith in Him is genuine and pure. I will make mention of you in my prayers and remember without ceasing your work of faith, and labor of love, and patience of hope in our Lord Jesus Christ.[3] Know that you may always return to my island to find rest for your soul."

Martine then felt the soft caress of numerous, blossom-laden vines. She turned around and saw the shrub vanish through the black door of that most peculiar shack. What happened next took her breath away: Millions of fireflies rose from the ground and surrounded the shack with countless points of twinkling light, and then the shack itself began to glow a deep, comforting ruby red. At that moment, the sun rose and painted the early morning sky with rich, vivid hues. Martine had no idea how much time had passed: It could be only seconds, or it could have been years. Time was of no importance on that little island, which appeared to stand outside of time and space.

Martine rose from her spot and walked back to the shore. The pelican accompanied her, and when its feet touched the land, he squawked and nodded its beak. He then turned around and went back to the island as Martine returned to the city.

What she found when she returned was a city she hardly recognized. It had grown in size and population; the noise and smell had increased, as well. She wandered the streets for hours until something familiar caught her eye, and then she could work her way back to the convent.

When she finally got there, Martine was stunned to see that it was boarded up and vacant; it looked deserted and forgotten. She received even more of a shock when she saw her reflection in a pane of glass. There before her was the reflection of someone she did not recognize: an exhausted woman whose attire was dusty and ragged. Martine looked over her shoulder to see who it could be but, with a stunning clarity, realized it was herself. Desperate to find out what had happened, she once again went from door to door, though this time she was not received as cordially as before. People assumed that she was one of the multitudes of the destitute who now littered the streets. New Orleans was a city she no longer recognized. Further, it seemed to be under some form of military occupation. This made no sense to her at all.

Exhausted and frightened, Martine made her way through the French Market, where she picked up bits of conversation. What she learned horrified her: The country was at war with itself! Those who called themselves the Union forces had captured New Orleans. They had taken control of the great port and then traveled up the river, where they established several military forts. Now, a ruthless man named General Benjamin Butler was in control, and he had placed the entire city under martial law.

"How could this be?" she asked herself. "How?"

Exhausted, confused, and alone, Martine wandered across the park and went into the St. Louis Cathedral, though it now looked very different from the one she remembered. She sat down in a pew, exhausted, and began to cry softly. Before too long, a venerable old sister approached and placed her hand upon Martine's shoulder.

"My dear," said the sister, "may I be of help?"

Martine turned around to see who it was and discovered, to her delight, that it was another nun.

"Oh, Sister," said Martine, "I don't know how you can. Nothing is as it should be."

"Since *they* arrived, *nothing* is as it should be," the old sister said, with just an ounce of acid in her voice.

"No, no, that's not what I mean. I don't even know how to explain it."

"Try, my dear, try," said the sister.

Martine told her everything. When she was finished, the old sister just stared at her, unable to comprehend the fantastic story. In particular was the huge age discrepancy, which should have made this mysterious woman far older than herself by many, many years, and yet she appeared to be no more than thirty years old.

The old sister, unable to comprehend what she had just heard, decided to put it aside and dwell on the present. She said, "Dear, we have a few little rooms in our house. Perhaps you should come with me. I'll see to it that you get something to eat, a bath, and a good night's sleep. After you're refreshed, you'll be able to think more clearly. Does that sound like something you would like?"

"Yes, yes it does," said a grateful Martine.

With that, the two rose from the pew. Sister Mary led Martine out of the cathedral through a back door and down an alley until they came to a secluded, vine-covered brick wall with a wrought iron gate. They went through the gate and into a stone-paved courtyard garden, an oasis in the midst of a very troubled, very noisy city. Within the courtyard, a moss-laden oak grew, surrounded by palm fronds, jasmine and moon vines, and azalea and magnolia blooming in abundance. The house, a two-storied brick structure with faded white trim, possessed a second-level balcony with tall glass windows, framed by full-length shutters, which overlooked an imported fountain.

The sister took Martine into the house, which was not ornate or ostentatious, but still quite comfortable and nicely appointed. Several religiously themed paintings hung on the walls, as well as a few beautiful sculptural objects placed prominently throughout.

They made their way up the staircase and down a hall, where the sister brought her to a small bedroom that overlooked the courtyard. The sister said, "I think you shall find that this room is most comfortable. Get settled, and I'll be back in a few minutes with a good meal for you. You will find a nightgown and robe hanging in the armoire. There is a fresh water pump and all you will need in the bathroom. By the time you've cleaned up and changed, I will be back with your meal. Will this be all right for you?"

"Oh, yes," said Martine, "thank you so much. Your kindness means more to me than you'll ever know."

Martine did just as the sister had suggested. In a very short time, she returned with a tray of food and a pot of tea. "Now dear," she said, "you eat and then get a good night's rest. You'll feel much better in the morning, and then we can have a nice long talk. God bless you." She left the room and quietly closed the door behind her.

After finishing her meal, Martine stretched out on the bed and within a few minutes was in a deep sleep, unaware that fireflies began settling outside of her window.

Martine had been asleep for several hours when the sound of hushed voices in the courtyard awakened her. She went to the window and, under the light of the full moon, saw several sisters ushering what appeared to be a large family of slaves across the courtyard. They kept looking over their shoulders, obviously terrified. The sisters stopped abruptly and pulled back a portion of the massive foliage that covered the courtyard wall to reveal a secret door, through which another nun emerged. She acknowledged the family and then led them through the door and out of sight. In a few moments, Martine heard hushed voices and footsteps ascend the stairs and pass by her room. She knew there was nothing to be done at this time, so she returned to bed and once again fell into a deep sleep.

Martine was awakened by a knock at the door. When she opened it, a young postulant stood with a fresh habit folded across her arms. She presented this to Martine and then invited her to join them for morning prayers in the courtyard, to be followed by breakfast in the dining hall. Martine eagerly accepted, looking forward to joining the sisters as they worshipped and offered prayers.

Unbeknownst to Martine, the Mother Superior had sent a messenger to the Ursuline convent to inquire about their guest. The response only deepened the mystery: There had been a Sister Martine, one of the original Ursulines, but that was over one hundred years ago! Surely, this woman who claimed to be Sister Martine must have suffered some calamity that would cause her to fabricate such an identity. The messenger advised them to treat her with all sympathy and charity, but to also be wary.

Martine joined the sisters in the courtyard and found that this time of prayer and worship was just what she needed to further refresh her soul and spirit. She followed them into the dining hall, where a simple but lovely meal had been prepared. Martine listened to their conversation as they made plans of the day, and she was delighted when they asked if she would like to be involved, to which she eagerly replied yes.

As the meal progressed, Martine felt more at ease, until a lull in conversation occurred. She then spoke up and said, "Sisters, last night something very odd occurred outside of my window. I was wondering ..."

But before she could finish her sentence, she noticed several of the sisters exchange conspiratorial glances.

"Martine," one of them said, "we were all fast asleep."

Another sister spoke up, adding, "Nothing happened, or otherwise we would have known."

"But I saw you, several of you, as you rushed across the courtyard with what must have been a slave family," said a confused Martine.

"Dear," said Mother Superior, "you were exhausted and utterly spent. There is no telling what you might have dreamt."

"I didn't dream it! I didn't!" she insisted.

"Come along, dear; everything will be fine, you'll see."

Martine realized that whatever had occurred, she would not discover what it was through this kind of discourse. She decided to forgo further questions but to keep an open eye for any further occurrences.

For the next several days, Martine worked alongside the other sisters and became a cherished asset to their endeavors: so much so, in fact, that Mother Superior invited her to stay indefinitely if she so desired (and, it should be noted, so that Mother Superior could keep her eye on this mystery who had begun to unfold and blossom before her eyes).

Late one night, after everyone had retired, Martine was once again awakened by the sound of hushed voices in the courtyard. When she rose from bed, she saw that around her window were an abundance of fireflies that cast a magical light into her room. She threw on her robe, quietly exited her room, stealthily descended the stairs, and entered the courtyard. She would have remained hidden in the shadows had not the fireflies surrounded her and given her away. The sisters, as well as the three slaves who were with them, froze in their tracks when they saw this incredible, incandescent sight. One of the sisters had the presence of mind to shush everyone as she grabbed Martine by the wrist and pulled her along with them.

Martine was led behind the vines, through the secret door, and down a narrow and dank stairway into a tunnel. Torches lined the walls, and one of the sisters took one and held it aloft. The tunnel went on for quite a ways until it led to another narrow stairway; they opened a door in the roof of the tunnel and then pushed the slaves through. The door was then shut from the outside, and all of the sisters returned to the house by the same path they had just taken. They emerged into the darkened courtyard and would have gone quietly back to their rooms had the fireflies not surrounded Martine once again.

In awe, the sisters moved back from her, made the sign of the cross, and then fled to their rooms. Martine was left alone in the courtyard, unobserved, or so she thought: Mother Superior had seen all that transpired from her balcony. She knew immediately that this was something not entirely of this world and that perhaps, just perhaps, Martine's story had more truth in it than she had given her credit for. Time would tell.

Over the next few weeks, nothing of great importance occurred. Martine had become a vital part of the convent's management and was beloved by all those with whom she worked and lived. She continued to possess an air of mystery when she would leave the convent on one of her long walks. Mother Superior took note and then one day, being one who was also blessed with an insatiable curiosity, decided to follow her.

Mother Superior kept a good distance from Martine, who never suspected that she was being followed. After a couple of hours, they were far outside the city perimeters and into the swamp country. Mother Superior was shocked when she noticed natives, whose skin was a lustrous red, emerge from the dense bayou, reverently nod their heads toward Martine, and then return to the protective cover of the swamp.

As if that was not enough, it came as a huge surprise to Mother Superior when Martine crossed over a rickety walkway toward a tiny island, sat down, took off her shoes, dangled her feet in the red waters, and was then joined by a pelican that, like an old familiar friend, sat down beside her. Martine then began a conversation with the pelican.

Mother Superior then noticed something that quite took her breath away: A blossom-covered shrub suddenly moved from one place to a spot directly behind Martine, and then a few laden vines actually caressed her, and she never flinched. Martine never turned around but shifted her conversation from the pelican to the shrub. Mother Superior was unable to catch her breath she was so stunned by what she saw.

Mother Superior was in for one more enormous shock: She heard a deep, melodious voice from within the shrub say, "Bring them here." Martine rose from her spot and, followed by the pelican, began to cross the walkway again. The shrub moved toward a flimsy shack, the door opened and closed, and then the whole shack glowed a deep ruby red. Mother Superior quickly made the sign of the cross.

Mother Superior returned her gaze toward Martine's direction and was rendered speechless: Martine was now surrounded and illuminated by millions of fireflies that transformed her into that strange vision she had seen in the courtyard. As Martine continued to walk, the light of the fireflies slowly diminished, and Mother Superior followed her home. Nothing was said at the time about the events of that evening, but Mother Superior kept a watchful eye upon this most unusual woman.

Several weeks passed, until one night, Martine heard a quiet rap on her door. She opened it and found two sisters, who took her by the hand and led her to the courtyard, where a few more sisters were clustered about another slave family. The sisters led them through the secret door and down the tunnel, only to find, in horror, that the door that led out had been sealed shut. Panicked, they returned to the courtyard, unsure what to do or whether their plans had been discovered. Mercifully, when they emerged, they were relieved to discover that they were safe ... for the moment.

The next morning at breakfast, the sisters confessed to Martine the truth of what had happened the night before. They believed that man must not own man as slaves, so they helped those who had been enslaved to escape their captivity. A secret network of people devoted to these unfortunates had been established throughout the South. As for the family they now hid within their walls, they must come up with a plan. Martine, without wasting a breath, said, "Trust them to me."

Late that night, Martine led the family along the secretive back alleys and swampy paths she had traveled for so long. Miraculously, there was a heavy fog that helped conceal them, and they never encountered a single individual. When at last they drew close to the pier, a single line of fireflies flew out meet them. Martine motioned for the family to follow, which they did, because they knew they had no other choice.

The family was apprehensive but did as Martine had told them. As they set foot on the island, the pelican appeared and nodded his head as if in approval. The door to the shack then opened, and as they entered, the shack began to glow with that beautiful red light Martine had so often seen and which had brought her so much comfort in the past. Then the song of the loon broke out and filled the night with joy.

Once Martine was sure the family was safe, she turned to leave and walked right into Mother Superior. "My dear," she said to Martine, "we must talk. Please tell me what this is all about. New Orleans has many, many mysteries and secrets, but this is something I do not comprehend at all."

Martine felt a wave of relief as she told Mother Superior of her many experiences on the island. When questioned about who lived there, Martine confessed that she was not entirely sure; he had never physically revealed himself so that she could see him. She was uncertain if he was an angel; perhaps he was some other kind of spiritual being that was altogether different from the angels. Martine told Mother Superior that he, like they, served the Most High God and His Son. She had also learned that his name was Adon Caddo; "Adon" was a title of sorts. There were many Adons who were sent to earth to watch over His chosen ones.

"But my dear," said a very perplexed Mother Superior, "how can you be sure this Adon Caddo is not an emissary of the evil one?"

"I wondered that very same thing until I realized everything he said always led to Christ. I've tried this spirit on numerous occasions, and every time he confessed with all certainty that Jesus is God, and that He came in the flesh and dwelt among us, that He died for our sins, and that He rose from the dead. And, as we know, the Word says that we are to recognize the Spirit of God by asking that very question, and that what is not of God is incapable of making such an admission."[4]

After careful consideration, Mother Superior admitted that it was true. "Then, my dear," she said to Martine, "we must thank God for this, this, this Adon Caddo. And though I do not fully understand why he is here, I cannot ignore the wonders that surround his presence, and how he has brought you into his work. But I have more questions for you." And, like a friend who has shared many secrets, she leaned into Martine and asked, "Have you ever been in that shack? What is it about that pelican? Where do those fireflies come from?"

"Mother Superior, I've never been in the shack. Truth be told, I've never been invited in. The pelican, however, has been as close a friend as one could ask for. The only thing I can tell you about the fireflies is that the path of the just is as the shining light that shines more and more until that perfect day.[5] They have lit my path on far too many dark occasions to carry out His will; other than that, I have no further explanation."

Mother Superior nodded and then entwined Martine's arm in hers as they walked home. When they arrived at the gate, they saw that everything was in turmoil. Mother Superior motioned for Martine to remain outside and entered the courtyard, to discover that the sisters were lined up against a wall; a military detachment stood in front of them. There was an imposing commander who viciously hurled a barrage of questions at them:

"Where did you take them? Where are they hidden? What have you done with them? We have ways of finding out!"

"Excuse me," Mother Superior said in her most imposing, sanctimonious voice, "why are you here? What is the meaning of this?"

"We are here because witnesses have claimed that your sisters are involved with aiding and abetting the escape of property that does not belong to you. What do you have to say for yourself?"

Mother Superior crossed herself and boldly stepped up to the commander; speaking with as much condescension as she could muster, she said, "Sir, I have not the slightest idea of what you are talking about. How is it possible for anyone to provide escape for a material possession?"

"You know precisely what I mean. To provide a means of escape for a slave is exactly the same thing as stealing property that belongs to another."

"So you say, Commander, so you say," Mother Superior said boldly. "Sir, let me tell you something: We have never, do you understand me, never done such a thing, nor will we ever be accused of such a crime. You are ill informed. People will confess to anything if enough … pressure is applied. I would suggest you have facts to present before you make any other vile accusation. Do you understand me? Now, please leave; you hinder our work."

As Mother Superior spoke, the other sisters noticed an unusual fog had begun to creep in through the gate, a fog that danced with tiny specks of light. Though their eyes widened, they did not betray their beloved Martine as she entered the courtyard and quietly slipped behind the vines and into the tunnel. The fireflies then swarmed the commander and quickly flew up and out of sight.

A fitting end to a nasty affair, thought Mother Superior.

The commander, as he attempted to remain unfazed, said, "To ensure that felonious, illicit, or prosecutable actions do not occur, I will leave a few of my men to protect both you and the other sisters."

"You do that," sneered Mother Superior, "you just do that." She then turned to the sisters and said sweetly, "Come now, we must prepare for our evening prayers."

The sisters followed Mother Superior into the house and left the guards in the courtyard.

In hushed, conspiratorial tones, the sisters met in the room they used as a chapel. Once they were all behind closed doors, a sister spoke up and said, "Mother Superior, we have ... another problem, if you know what I mean." She then cast a glance toward the window that looked out toward the vine-covered wall.

Mother Superior followed her gaze, crossed herself, and then said, "We shall pray for God's direction." The sisters all fell to their knees and began to pray. All, that is, except Martine, who spoke up and said, "Mother Superior, I have that friend who could help us. I'm sure he would."

"You are right, my dear," Mother Superior said. "Just like Esther, for such a time as this, yes?"[6]

Later that night, the sisters quietly went to the courtyard. The guards had fallen asleep at their posts. A few sisters went to the wall, uncovered the door, and opened it. From within emerged another terrified slave family of a father, mother, and three children. Without making a sound, the family followed Martine and a few of the sisters out of the gate and down the alley. Martine led them on the path she had so frequently taken, keeping everyone in the darkest shadows.

They reached the outskirts of the city and began to walk the familiar swampy paths.

Since New Orleans was under martial law, there were guards stationed along the way, something Martine was all too aware of. What she and the other sisters were not aware of was that there were patrols that cruised the bayous throughout the swamps. Their specific purpose was to capture malefactors, traitors, spies, and runaways.

When the Black Gardenia was finally in sight, Martine began to pick up the pace. The youngest child was unable to keep up; she tripped and fell, letting out an unintentional scream of pain.

As her voice echoed throughout the swamp, a patrol was nearby, and a soldier shouted, "Halt! Who goes there?"

With freedom in sight for the family, Martine yelled, "Follow me! Run!"

The family and the sisters did just as she said. They could clearly hear the sounds of soldiers and dogs getting closer and closer.

When Martine finally reached the walkway, something incredible happened: The fireflies formed a path of light. Martine stood at the edge as she frantically motioned the family and the other sisters across the walkway. At the island end of the walkway, the pelican hovered overhead, and the mysterious shack began to glow.

The sound of barking dogs and soldiers pierced the night. The family and sisters made it across the walkway, but as Martine shouted for the family to go into the shack, a shot rang out, hitting her in the back. As she fell, the fireflies swarmed beneath her and carried her onto the island; as that strange door opened, she was engulfed in light and taken into the shack.

These events did not, however, stop the soldiers, who continued to follow. As they approached the walkway, they were halted in their tracks by a huge whirlwind, out of which rose a glowing red form that towered above them. The form thrust out its right arm; a bolt of crimson light then rushed toward the soldiers, engulfing them. It immobilized them and forced them to their knees. At the same time, the form opened wide its mouth and spoke with a voice like thunder, yelling, *"No!"*

The soldiers covered their ears and bent low to the ground.

As the wind rushed around the soldiers, the sisters, stunned by all they had seen, ran across the walkway, past the immobilized soldiers, and returned to the city. The last thing they heard was the song of the loon.

Martine awoke, if that's what she truly did, at the base of a golden stairway that seemed to stretch endlessly in both directions. The stairway was composed of innumerable golden threads. In the far distance, at the end of each thread, a flash of light would occur, out of which a person would appear. Each person would ascend toward twelve giant gates that were made of pearl. At the top of each pearl, a name was inscribed. A river, clear as diamonds, flowed through each of the gates. Each river cascaded down its own path carved into the golden stairs, and each glowed with the light of one of the twelve colors that corresponded to the stones of foundation.

Martine never questioned that she was to ascend; she had already begun, as did the countless others who each appeared from a flash of light. She glowed with the subtle iridescence of every rainbow color.

Martine rose upwards toward a great translucent wall that shimmered and glistened as the finest crystal. The foundation of the great wall was composed of twelve strata of precious stones.

When Martine arrived at her gate, she discovered that, far off in the distance, the rivers joined with nine others and became the one Great River. The Great River was clear as crystal, and on either side was the tree of life, which bore twelve manner of fruits.[7] Each side of the Great River was paved in gold as clear as glass, in which every species of flower continuously bloomed and never withered or saw corruption.

Martine passed through the gate and realized that the air, if that truly was what it could be, pulsated with the sound of music, and that it was indescribably sweet.

As she tried to absorb all that she experienced, she felt her hand gently grasped. "It's you," she said.

She then heard a lovely voice that simply said, "Welcome home."

CHAPTER 6

PEARL

On the hot summer night that Pearlipatta de la Bouchard was born, her mother died; she had been an ardent fan of the writings of that eccentric Dane, E.T.A. Hoffman, hence the name Pearlipatta (his unfortunate creation cursed by the evil Mouse Queen). Considered royalty at the Palace of Mirrors, the most prestigious house de la nuit in New Orleans, Pearlipatta's mother had been a well-known damsel. Time spent in her company would cost upwards of $1,000. In the nineteenth century, this was a king's ransom, yet there were many who would gladly pay the price.

Known as "Pearl," she was raised by the twenty-four other women who also resided in the Palace of Mirrors. They were joined by an assortment of slaves, hired hands, musicians, cooks, and most of all, Madame Bellavance (Belle, to her closest intimates), the owner of the Palace.

Madame had been a very famous Parisian courtesan in her day; she had amassed quite a sizable fortune before political necessity required her immediate departure from the City of Lights (she knew far too much about far too many people). After a lengthy, covert voyage, she ended up in the French Quarter of New Orleans. From the moment her foot touched the ground, Madame knew she had found her home. She immediately sought a sumptuous *grande maison* in the

Quarter and, when the renovations peculiar to her form of enterprise were accomplished, took to staffing her new house.

Madame was very particular; only the finest of the fine young women would do. She was most discriminating in her choice of employees; she had her reputation to consider, after all. Madame took good care of her girls, but if there were ever the slightest trace of disloyalty, dishonesty, or disease, the brunt of her formidable wrath would be felt immediately. There were numerous young women who thought they could get the upper hand with Madame, and there were numerous young women who were ruined for life as a result. For all intent and purpose, all those in Madame's employ were actually slaves of varying degree.

Accidents did happen, and to those whose loyalty and dedication to Madame had never been questioned, she would do everything she could to help. Such was the case with Pearl's mother, a woman Madame virtually thought of as her own daughter. When Pearl was born, she became the de facto granddaughter of Madame, though, as she was to learn, she was actually nothing more than a very pampered possession, a thing.

Pearl enjoyed a happy, if isolated, childhood, and though she had never been permitted outside the formidable stone and brick walls that encircled the Palace, everyone loved her and thought of her as their pet. As she grew, it became obvious that not only had she inherited her mother's great beauty. Pearl also had an intelligently winsome, almost ethereal personality that was carried by lithe, long limbs. Pearl did not walk; she glided. Further, her lengthy and ravishing brunette locks framed a porcelain complexion accentuated by red lips, naturally blushed cheekbones, and stunning green eyes that peered out through extraordinarily long, dark lashes. She received no formal education, but she was certainly quite intelligent and eager to learn. By the time Pearl was ten, she was fluent in English, French, Spanish, German, and Creole. She was also quite accomplished on both the harpsichord and piano. Madame was no fool; she had personally seen that Pearl received the finest training one could acquire in the

Quarter because she would eventually become her cherished prize, her most lucrative possession.

When Pearl turned ten years old, Madame began to take her on short jaunts into the Quarter and the French Market. Heads turned as these two extraordinary beauties passed by. These excursions were Madame's method of advertising her most valuable, upcoming asset. This new asset was certainly noticed, particularly by the circle of wealthy merchants, bankers, and plantation owners who had been known to frequent the Palace.

As they walked, Pearl and Madame ignored everyone, and with their heads proudly held aloft, they would go about their business (though the business Pearl assumed they were on was not the business Madame conducted). Pearl was, after all, Madame's property, and it was time for Madame to get a return on her considerable investment.

When Pearl turned twelve, she found the Palace in a state of great enthusiasm and excitement. She was unable to discern the cause for such festivities, until one of the slave children she had befriended came to her one night and, with a conspiratorial glance, took Pearl by the hand and ever so quietly led her to a window that opened into Madam's apartments. There she heard the melodious voice of Madame address four of her most trusted girls.

"Ladies," said Madame, "the time has come for Pearl to make her entrance into our society. I have been promised an enormous sum from a gentleman who wishes to purchase her first night. I intend to make this the most lavish event the Palace has ever hosted. I have hired the finest seamstresses in New Orleans to create new gowns for each of you; you must look your best. We will cater the most sumptuous of feasts and hire the finest musicians. When the time arrives, I will have Pearl brought to him borne aloft upon a golden litter, carried by four Nubians. This will be the event of the year; absolutely nothing can go wrong. Do you understand me? Each of you will be responsible for her womanly education. Though she will be presented to him chaste and innocent, she must be aware of the most subtle means to induce his pleasure."

Pearl, horrified, could not believe what she had heard. She then realized that she meant nothing to Madame, other than a means to make a profit. Her world disintegrated before her. Pearl knew she could never go through with this plan; she must escape from the Palace immediately. So she did the only thing she could think of, she ran. She ran into the depths of night's darkness in a secretive city of alleys, shady walks, and hidden dangers.

As Pearl made her escape, she muttered prayers to whatever deity would take pity upon her. A firefly suddenly caught her attention, and for whatever reason, she followed it into the courtyard of a tiny church. Pearl entered a small chamber, illuminated by several candles. At the front was a long table over which hung a cross with the image of a suffering man nailed upon it. Pearl figured that he was in far worse condition than she, therefore, he must possess some higher power she knew nothing about. She begged him to help her, but just as she finished her dialogue, the firefly reappeared, flew around her head, and then exited. Pearl instinctively followed.

New Orleans, a sleepless city, forced Pearl to be as invisible as possible. She clung to the shadows and never allowed herself to be seen in the open. It took her many hours, but she finally made it out of the city and into the surrounding swamplands. Surprisingly, the firefly continued in front of her.

Pearl was more convinced than ever that its intention was to lead her. "But where?" she pondered. Did it matter? Really, what did she have to lose if she continued to follow it?

Scared, exhausted, lonely, lost, and desperately hungry, Pearl could take no more. She sat down under the shade of a giant, moss-covered oak that stood beside a small bayou and began to cry. She then fell asleep and did not awaken until very late in the night.

During the night, she awoke, rubbed the sleep from her eyes, and glanced heavenward. What she saw took her breath away. Above her head was what appeared to be a profuse canopy of stars that joyfully twinkled in the night sky. Their beauty overcame her until she noticed that they began to descend round about her.

It was then that she heard a still, small voice whisper to her soul, "This is the way, walk in it."[8]

She looked to see who spoke to her but saw no one except an old pelican, which turned away from her and waddled onto a wooden pier outlined by the light of thousands of fireflies. It waddled across the water and onto a tiny island on which stood a rickety shack that was engulfed by the most aromatic vines of extraordinary black blossoms.

Pearl had a choice: She could either continue her journey on the dusty road, or as bizarre as it was, she could follow that voice and cross the water toward the shack. She stood up, brushed herself off, and ventured across the walkway, surrounded by fireflies.

When she had crossed the water, she noticed that there was an inner red glow that shone through the cracks of the shack's walls. Pearl pondered this oddity until the door slowly, invitingly, opened and beckoned her to enter. Again, she had a choice to make: should she enter or should she go? It was her decision alone to make. Once again, she relied on instinct: She entered.

The first thing that happened was that a staircase stretched down before her. As she descended the stairs, the walls began to glow and shimmer with an incandescent blue light. This light was reflected and refracted by thousands of crystal chandeliers and mirrors, reminiscent of those in the Palace of Mirrors.

As Pearl continued downward, she saw translucent, swirling images of people she had known at the Palace, as well as many she did not recognize. They were all in a state of festive celebration. Pearl could practically feel their touch, so real did they seem.

Suddenly, a loud cheer arose from this miasma of translucent beings, and there before her was a beautiful child, carried aloft on an enormous golden platter, a dish to be served. This ethereal child was then lowered to the floor and walked directly through Pearl. The child was then led to a horrific horned beast of tremendous proportions. Pearl, horrified, screamed and ran as fast as she could. She found no exit as the images, the walls, and the chandeliers all began to swirl about her.

As Pearl ran, she heard a knocking sound. Ahead of her, a door appeared. She did not hesitate to run to it. She turned the knob and opened the door. Before her stood a man who resembled the man hanging on the cross she had seen earlier.

He stretched out his hand and said, "I stood at your door and knocked.[9] You were predestined to be my adopted child. Come, walk with me to my Father's house."

Overwhelmed and at peace, Pearl placed her hand in His and walked away with him. The beautiful sound of the common loon was then heard across the swamp.

CHAPTER 7
CATIA RENATA

After France had ceded New Orleans to the Spanish in 1763, the influx of new cultures upon this melting pot of a port city was palpable. By the 1820s, New Orleans had become a rich, vibrant, multicultural city known as the Jewel of the South. Whereas racism and bigotry plagued other major cities, New Orleans was unique. Every race represented had the ability of social and financial advancement.

As the prosperity of New Orleans grew, so did the influence of the Catholic Church, as evidenced by the presence of the Capuchins, Jesuits, and Ursulines. Each order sought to enrich the lives of the inhabitants and to convert the lost of the city and the native populations.

The Capuchins, a branch of the Franciscans, sought a more ascetic form of existence through a return to a primitive life of solitude and penance. They devoted themselves to their unbridled passion for God through the elimination of all earthly desire. They believed that only through self-induced mortification of the flesh could their entrance into heaven be ensured. The higher church authorities did not approve of their practices and sought to arrest them for abandoning their churchly duties. The Capuchins were either forced into hiding or relocated.

Among the Capuchins was Friar Sebastian de las Casas. His practice and dedication was even more devout and severe than what was common amongst the order. The dedication and devotion of the other practitioners paled when compared to the extent that Friar Sebastian conducted his daily ritual. He was rigid in his beliefs and acknowledged that there was no shadow of turning where his righteousness was concerned. As a result, Friar Sebastian lived an isolated life and was rarely disturbed.

Misunderstood and persecuted by his own church, Friar Sebastian realized he had no alternative but to flee from his home in Cadiz if he wanted to pursue his particularly strict path of righteousness. With no room for any form of corruption within the church, himself, or anyone else, Friar Sebastian chose to venture to the New World, where a Capuchin order had been established outside of New Orleans. His naïveté and arrogance convinced him that in the New World, things must surely exist in a purer state; therefore, he could devote himself to a chaste life free of worldly distractions.

During the lengthy voyage, Friar Sebastian intermingled with the crew of ruffians who managed the ship. True to his calling, he attempted to convert those lost souls, to no avail. They would have nothing to do with him.

During the endless weeks at sea, Friar Sebastian overheard many extraordinary things. Chief among these were frequent references about a woman named Catia Renata. Though unfazed by the crew's lustful comments, their insistence that she was the most beautiful woman on earth enabled a shard of curiosity, intermingled with a hint of intrigue, to catch the attention of the friar. He could not understand how they could be so enamored by such an individual whom they had never met nor, from what he surmised, would they ever have the opportunity to meet, given their paltry condition.

Finally, after what seemed an eternity, the ship that carried Friar Sebastian pulled into the raucous Port of New Orleans. Expecting a utopia, he soon realized that he had grossly misjudged the purity of the New World. As he wandered the chaotic streets, what met his eyes was a city more corrupt and vice-laden than anything he had ever seen in Cadiz. Chagrined and bitterly disappointed, Friar Sebastian finally found refuge at the Capuchin monastery outside of the city.

As he settled into his new surroundings, Friar Sebastian began to take long walks through the city to satiate his curiosity about what was now a city buried in the depths of sin and depravity, a city of vice, intrigue, and dark secrets. He told himself that there was no better place for him to wage a holy war against the rampant corruption. This became his sole purpose: the conversion of the lost.

While upon one of his holy walks, Friar Sebastian noticed a group of prosperous merchants and businessmen, whose attention was fixated upon the most extraordinary woman he had ever seen. Quite tall and statuesque, she had breathtaking chestnut hair that was piled high upon her head in an abundance of cascading curls, topped off by a large-brimmed white straw hat, accentuated with pale peach roses. Her white linen gown, adorned with peach and white ribbons and flowers, intentionally focused attention upon her provocative form.

Upon her long, graceful neck, she wore a multi-strand pearl necklace. Matching earrings hung on either side of her beautiful face. Her stunning caramel complexion emphasized high cheekbones, full red lips, and piercing green eyes that peered at the world through lush, thick lashes. She was an amalgam of every culture represented in New Orleans. She did not walk but floated as she engaged in conversations with her throng of entranced, hopeless admirers. Her voice was melodic. It was no wonder she was pursued.

Friar Sebastian was well aware of the women of Cadiz and the nightly trade they plied on the streets. This woman, however, was totally unique and utterly different. In the full light of day, she was astonishingly beautiful beyond description. Friar Sebastian had never seen the likes of her before. At that moment, he believed he had been brought to the New World for one reason, and one reason only: He would, he must, convert this ravishingly lost woman to the way of the cross so that her immortal soul would not be banished to everlasting perdition.

As Friar Sebastian pondered his new cause, the woman happened to glance in his direction, and for a brief second, their eyes met. At that moment, Friar Sebastian was rocked to his very core. He realized that there was no time to waste; he must minister to this lost soul. But how, he wondered.

Without drawing attention to himself, Friar Sebastian began to conduct a subtle investigation into just whom this woman could be. On the pretense that he was in search of those who needed to hear his message, Friar Sebastian began to frequent the streets of the city during the evenings and well into the night. Though he encountered any number of scurrilous individuals, the beautiful woman eluded him until, late one night a particularly rowdy crowd accidentally swept him into their merry group and into one of the beautiful mansions that lined the streets.

When Friar Sebastian caught his breath, he discovered that he was in a room that could rival any in Cadiz. Numerous crystal chandeliers, suspended from very high ceilings, cast a golden glow. Floor-to-ceiling windows, draped in *poitier* of heavy rose silk brocade, were opened to allow the entrance of the fragrantly aromatic evening breeze. Between the windows were floor-to-ceiling mirrors, framed with gold that reflected the grandeur of the room. Giant vases containing fantastic floral displays punctuated the room. Along one wall was a sumptuous buffet with more offerings than Friar Sebastian had ever seen. The room was filled with men and women, all sumptuously attired and convinced that this was the most important moment of their lives. At the far end of the room, a grand staircase descended from the upper level. A small orchestra accompanied the entire spectacle.

Friar Sebastian, whose attention had been arrested by a mirror's reflection, suddenly noticed a woman of ravishing beauty descending the stairs. It was she! Their eyes briefly met once again, and then, in a swirl of frivolous lasciviousness, she was gone.

A man standing next to Friar Sebastian lifted his champagne glass toward her and said, "Ah, Catia, if only you were mine." He exhaled as one who realized that the prize he so desperately desired would always be out of his reach. He drank his champagne with abject resignation and then left, totally unaware that the strange man in black monk robes had heard every word.

"Catia," whispered Friar Sebastian, "how beautiful a name, and yet how ironic to think that her name means chaste and pure. God Himself brought me to this wasteland. Her shame, and the incredible harm she has caused, has bitterly distressed my soul. I vow that I will win her soul to God."

Friar Sebastian hastily exited through a side door and found himself in an exquisite courtyard garden. Overcome, he sat on a wrought iron settee and prayed, "Lord God Almighty, my soul is in Your hands. Do with me as You will. I will deliver this woman from her fleshly servitude. I will give her to You. I will bring her back from perdition."

Friar Sebastian was distracted from his prayer when he heard the melodious laughter of Catia, pursued by numerous suitors. She suddenly stopped and turned her gaze upon the friar. Again, their eyes met, but she then did something totally unexpected: She laughed ... directly at him. The suitors, unaware of this strange man, continued their futile pursuit. Then she was gone, no more than the memory of an enticing vision.

Friar Sebastian made his way out to the streets and began the long walk back to the monastery, though he was in such a daze that when he arrived, he passed it by and continued walking. He wandered into a bayou, and after a considerable time had passed, he noticed a small island upon which was a most unusual structure. Friar Sebastian then noticed a small pier that led to the island. Upon the pier was a pelican; when it saw Friar Sebastian, the bird turned and waddled to the shack.

Friar Sebastian then became aware of the island's overwhelming fragrance; after a few inhalations, it caused him to lose all strength. He abruptly sat upon the ground; his heart raced, and his mind was a jumble of new and strange thoughts.

Suddenly, to his astonishment, he heard a voice behind him, saying, "Do not consort with the spirit that controls her. It will engulf you and lead you to ruin."

Friar Sebastian quickly turned around to discover the source of the voice, but there was no one there except for the pelican, which simply stared at him, and a miasma of fireflies, whose illumination cast a magical light upon this very odd location.

Exhausted, Friar Sebastian stretched out on the ground and uttered a prayer: "I will call upon Your name, though these waters might rise and engulf me. Amen." He then fell into a deep slumber.

Friar Sebastian was awakened with the sun in his face and the sound of children's laughter. He sat up and saw several native children, who were pointing at him and laughing. He figured that he must be quite a sight to them, dressed as he was, so he joined in their laughter, until he saw an elderly woman walk toward the shack and place an offering of wildflowers at the threshold. She then gathered the children and walked across the pier and down the dirt road.

Friar Sebastian sat there, more confused than ever. He realized that there was something most unusual about this tiny island, but precisely what that could be, he had no idea. He would begin his own research into this mystery; perhaps it might even rid his mind of the memory of Catia.

Friar Sebastian returned to the monastery. Even though he remained silent about the events of the previous evening, he began to ask people about the island. Information was not abundant; people who knew about the island chose to shun it and leave it alone. There were a few people, however, who were convinced that a great healing spirit lived there and that the natives, who never wanted to offend such a spirit, left offerings as a form of worship and appeasement.

Weeks passed, and Friar Sebastian kept himself quite busy with the needs of the monastery. During this time, he was able to push any thoughts of Catia out of his mind. This was to change upon an excursion to the French Market.

Friar Sebastian wandered the bustling lanes that were stocked with every imaginable delicacy. As he reached for a fresh baguette, his hand brushed that of another customer. When he looked up, the first thing he saw were emerald eyes that looked at him through lush, dark lashes. It was Catia, as breathtaking as he remembered her. Her eyes remained fixed upon his.

"My goodness," a startled Catia said to Sebastian, "who could this stranger be, whose eyes pierce to the depths of my soul?"

"I know who you are, Madame. I must harden my heart against you to protect my own soul," an embarrassed Friar Sebastian replied.

Catia's eyes remained fixed upon his as she said, "Here now, is that how you would greet someone you hardly know? Come, let us walk together along the river and see how our conversation develops."

So overcome by her invitation, Friar Sebastian could do nothing but obey; they left the French Market and walked toward the river. Along the way, they passed several fashionable shops. Friar Sebastian thought that Catia would want to enter each shop, but they appeared to hold no interest for her. They came to a shop with an ornate gilt mirror in the window. Friar Sebastian noticed that when Catia caught a glimpse of her reflection, she turned quite pale. She regained her composure and then continued to walk.

"Father, tell me," Catia said sincerely, "why do I feel you despise me? What have I ever done to hurt you?"

"May I call you Catia?" asked Friar Sebastian. She nodded an assent. He continued, "I've watched you. You are a lure to the soul of man. Though you believe in love of the flesh, you are an avenue to perdition to those you seduce. You believe in love, but you condemn those who follow you to certain damnation. You do not realize that you are on the brink of utter desolation. You are one step away from being damned for all eternity. It is the grace of God alone that has kept your foot from slipping. It is His love for you. Do you not know? Do you not care?"

"Father," she said, "what makes you so severe? Why stifle the flame before your eyes? What a fool you are to forbid love. I believe only in love; nothing can swerve me. You have not tasted life; you know nothing of love."

"I loathe your false intoxications," said an irate Friar Sebastian. "I shall vanquish the enemy of your soul."

"We have reached my destination, Father. I shall take my leave of you now. Good day." With that, Catia crossed the street and went into her home, the very structure Friar Sebastian had entered many weeks ago.

Though he had no way to know, Friar Sebastian's words had cut Catia to the core. For the next several weeks, she existed in a morose state; she rarely left her home. Her focus returned over and over to her visage that she caught in that storefront window. For now, she knew that her appearance would carry her through. But, she wondered, what would happen when her beauty faded? What would happen when the frivolities of her existence ceased? She had already begun to experience an emptiness of soul, but now this emptiness began to threaten her, as if she stood on a precipice and stared down into an abyss. Catia began to question the words of Friar Sebastian. Did he really speak of a higher life; one that was attainable now and that would carry her into an eternity of love?

At the monastery, Friar Sebastian endured a torment of the soul. Night after night, he cried out to God, "Lord, shield my eyes from her beauty. Let me only see the beauty of her soul reborn."

Late one night, unable to sleep, Friar Sebastian decided to walk. For what seemed like hours, he wandered through the city and eventually ended up in the park in front of the St. Louis Cathedral.

Unbeknownst to him, Catia, too, had grown weary and restless. Under a full moon, she strolled those streets that were so familiar to her, only to find dissatisfaction at every corner. She entered a side door of the St. Louis Cathedral and stared in wonder at the artwork that depicted the risen Savior. Overwhelmed, she exited through the front doors and entered the park, where she noticed a man dressed in a black robe, sitting on a bench with his head in his hands. She knew immediately that it was Friar Sebastian. She quietly walked to him and gently sat next to him. Startled, he turned his head and saw that it was Catia. Before he could say anything, she raised her finger before her mouth to indicate that he should remain silent.

"Father," she whispered, "my soul is deeply disturbed. Tell me of this everlasting love you profess."

"I curse the living death that possesses you," he said.

"Do not despise me, Father. I did not choose this beauty. How could I? My soul, though, is barren and desperately empty. I can no longer endure in this condition. I so fear death. Father, what must I do?"

Friar Sebastian responded, "You can choose to live as a bride of the one who was your enemy, Christ. Only in this way will you know everlasting joy and peace."

Catia was silent. Friar Sebastian could see on her face the struggle she endured. Suddenly, she looked up, and he could see in her green eyes that something miraculous had occurred.

"Oh, Father," she cried, "something has happened to my ravaged soul! I am overwhelmed, overcome! What power is this that could so transform me in an instant? What am I to do?"

"There is a convent outside the city where the sisters will take care of you and guide you. I can take you there. But first, you must destroy all elements of your previous life, since they no longer maintain a hold upon you."

Together, they returned to her house. To Friar Sebastian's astonishment, Catia set her home ablaze. They then fled the city and went to the convent he had mentioned. The sisters greeted her with open arms and led her inside.

Friar Sebastian returned to the monastery where, at first, he felt pride and satisfaction for converting Catia. This he shared with his brothers in the monastery. After much time had passed, he realized that Catia still haunted him; his soul was deeply disturbed.

The Capuchin brothers began to notice that Sebastian had not eaten anything in weeks. They believed that the triumph he celebrated over Catia's conversion had broken him completely. What they did not realize was that, though he was broken, it was not for the reasons they surmised. He was broken because he finally realized that he was deeply in love with Catia. This was a torment such as he had never known, and it rocked him to his core.

During this time, an epidemic had broken out in New Orleans called, among several names, the Yellow Death, Yellow Jack, or the Yellow Plague; this disease chose no favorites, and everyone was a potential victim. Catia was no exception. As part of her new duties, she helped those who suffered and died. She gave no thought to herself and, in so doing, contracted the fatal disease.

Word of Catia's illness reached Friar Sebastian, and he rushed to the convent. When he saw her, though her beauty had not yet been affected, he could see she was in such a weakened condition that death certainly would call upon her shortly. He remembered what the natives had said about that peculiar little island he had happened upon. In that moment, to the protestations of the sisters, he swept Catia up in his arms and carried her to the island, where he attempted to minister to her in the hope that whatever power existed there would heal her and return her to him.

"Catia, Catia!" he cried. "You cannot leave me. All this time, I've lied to you. I am so desperately in love with you, nothing else matters. Nothing exists but my love for you. There is no truth except for the all-consuming love I have for you. Everything else is a lie. Everything."

With great effort, Catia lifted her arm and pointed toward the door of the shack that, at that moment, slowly began to open. Sebastian looked toward the direction she pointed and said, "My darling, what is it? What do you see?"

In ecstasy, she cried out, "I see the gates of heaven! They are open to me!" She rose up further and said, "I hear the music from within played by the angels!" Catia then rose out of Sebastian's arms and hovered in the air. As she floated toward the open door, she cried, "I see the face of Him who loves my soul!" With that last exclamation, Catia vanished inside the shack. Sebastian ran toward the door, but it slammed shut, prohibiting him entrance.

One more time, he heard that mysterious voice, saying, "I warned you not to consort with the spirit that controls her. Did I not tell you that it would engulf you and lead to your ruin? This way is barred from you. It is now up to you to work out your own salvation with fear and trembling."[10]

Sebastian was suddenly engulfed in a great swarm of luminescent fireflies and then left completely, and soul-shatteringly, alone. The sun eventually rose upon his desolation.

CHAPTER 8

THE VOODOO KING

The mystique of that little island, combined with its most strange inhabitant, developed into legend. The passing of time transformed the legend into myth. To live so close to something as shrouded in mystery as the Black Gardenia caused the superstitious natives to have a reverent fear of the island; finally, they avoided it completely. Word of its power, however, did filter back to the city, where practitioners of the black arts sought it out for the secrets it contained, in the vain hope that they could assume its power for their own profit.

Such an individual was Charles Beauregard de la Tour, the natural son of a free Creole woman and New Orleans businessman, Beauregard Vincent de la Tour. Though Charles' business was import-exports, this was a mere facade that enabled him to mask his true intention: the financial control of thousands of people whom he made dependent upon his services. These services were cunningly developed over the years through his association with the religious beliefs and customs of the African and Haitian immigrants brought to New Orleans, as well as a twisted version of the rites and rituals of the Catholic Church. This was nothing short of the full expression of the black arts, voodoo, through the use of calculated manipulation with showmanship flair. His power, vanity, and greed enabled him to declare himself the Voodoo King; hence, his nom de plume: King Charles.

King Charles was able to exert such powerful control through his manipulation of the most basic of human emotions: fear. He did this through his network of informants and thugs, who kept a very close watch and reported every detail of life in the French Quarter to him. Nothing happened that King Charles was not aware of, and that would in some fashion enable him to receive a substantial profit. It did not matter how many lives came in harm's way, or how much blood was shed, just as long as King Charles could cash in on their fear and misery.

Superstitious belief in powerful spirits, and the practice of magic, was rampant in nineteenth-century New Orleans. King Charles capitalized and profited on this. Over the years, he amassed a great fortune.

Another major asset that enabled him to gain such wealth and control was his appearance. He stood six foot five inches and was bone thin, with a wild shock of matted golden hair, eyes that coldly blazed with the light of an emerald, and a basso profundo voice. He always wore black suits that were made for him by an Italian tailor, tragically indebted to him. The suits were always accentuated with a single white gardenia boutonnière. His shirts were imported silk with either ivory or pearl buttons. About his neck he wore a silk cravat, usually blood red, that was held in place by a huge diamond. His long, bony fingers sported several gold and jeweled rings. And though he did not need it, he walked with an ebony cane inlaid with mother of pearl that concealed a sword of rapier strength and sharpness.

The most striking (and quite disturbing) feature of King Charles was that he was an albino, inherited from his mother's side, which caused him to be nearly 100 percent sunlight intolerant. As a result, he was rarely was seen in the light of day. When seen, his appearance was otherworldly, alien. Rumors were rampant about who, or what, he actually was. If met on the street, in the shadow of night, he could strike terror in the strongest of men.

At the height of his power, King Charles would put his voice to seductively hypnotic use, as he conducted voodoo rituals late at night along the banks of the Mississippi River. The segments of his rituals were highly organized and could be sequentially identified: 1. the song of preparation; 2. the song of invocation; 3. the song of possession; and 4. the song of farewell. The songs he sang were deliberate, elaborate, and descriptive portraits of the various deities he worshipped. The songs were sung to explain the deities' origins, powers, strengths, and weaknesses so that the practitioners would know how to attack or defend themselves against the spirits (of course, under the guidance of King Charles, for a hefty sum).

King Charles always claimed he first heard his songs in a dream or when he was possessed during a trance, when he claimed the song came directly from a spirit. Many of his songs intentionally sought to confuse the worshippers through the use of familiar Catholic tunes and the association of the Catholic saints with the voodoo deities.

King Charles was many things to many people. The one thing that linked it all together was, quite simply, that he was an errant fraud and a charlatan of extravagant and extraordinary abilities. His bluster so convinced the masses that he ruled virtually all of the New Orleans underground. They feverishly assembled on the banks for his midnight services, a *cause célèbre* attended by thousands. His popularity became so enormous that he was able to pull even the faithful to his shores and to their knees.

It was at one of those midnight services, as the drums hypnotized the worshippers, that King Charles first noticed something slightly amiss, something ... not quite right, something certainly not in accordance with his concept of reality. It was ever so slight; a person with a lesser mind would not have given it a second thought. King Charles was not that person of a lesser mind. He was suddenly, and for the first time in his life, utterly confounded ... and totally entranced. A black blossom with a mesmeric aroma hovered before his eyes. King Charles reached out with his bony hand to grasp it, but it was carried aloft on the wings of dozens of fireflies in full illumination. As mysteriously as it had appeared, it was gone.

King Charles was totally flummoxed. His green eyes had seen

something completely unattainable. He had no way to even search for it because he really did not know what "it" had been. For the next week, he was haunted, distracted, and completely consumed by the lingering memory of the fragrant blossom. Even when his informants came to him with valuable tidbits of manipulative information, he would simply wave them away.

A week passed, and once again, it was time for him to stage another service on the river's bank. At the height of the service, as the worshippers chanted and the drums beat ferociously, King Charles made his entrance. He strode up to his platform (a makeshift stage built above the waters of the Mississippi that stood high on wooden stilts and was accessed by a walkway). He turned to face the crowd but froze, unable to do a thing. There before him hovered the black blossom. With an involuntary, almost spastic, motion, his right hand bolted up and pointed to the flower.

His hand trembled and shook as his basso profundo voice boomed, "It's there! It's there!" Everyone looked in the direction he pointed but saw nothing. "Can you not see it? Tell me, can you see it? Tell me!" he roared.

The crowd, all too aware of the retribution their denial could bring, fell upon their faces as they moaned and wailed in mock worship and possession.

"Fools!" he shouted. "It is right there, a black flower, right there!"

The blossom then began to move away from him, floating through the frenzied worshippers. King Charles could do nothing but follow. He pushed his way through the crowd as he attempted to grasp it, but the flower was always just out of reach. Then, once again, it rose into the air, borne aloft by myriad illuminated fireflies, and vanished.

King Charles stood there, trembling with rage and frustration. When he regained his composure, he turned his back and simply walked away from the gathering. He wandered the streets, like a ghost in a daze. Those who saw him thought that he was in a deep trance and stepped out of his way.

As the sun began to rise, King Charles finally returned home.

He went into his lush bedroom and shut the heavy silk drapes. He then entered his bathroom and undressed for his bath. A sound came from his bedroom, a sound he did not recognize. He returned to the bedroom and discovered an antique crystal vase; it held a single black gardenia on the antique, gilt-encrusted, Louis XIV table. He cautiously walked toward it, leaned forward to inhale the aroma, and was knocked over and rendered unconscious by its fragrance. In this state, he dreamed a dream that would change his life. He saw a glowing red figure that towered over a swamp.

The figure said to him, "Find me," in a voice that spoke to every cell of his decrepit person.

King Charles remained in this stupefied condition for several days. Those who attended him were too terrified to come near for fear that they would disturb his communication with the spirit world. One brave soul built up the courage to pull one of the imported white sheets off of his bed and covered him with it.

When King Charles finally returned to this world, he simply stood up, wrapped the sheet about him, and walked out of his house, ignorant of anyone passing by. He walked and walked, to the outskirts of the city, down the Mississippi, then down a bayou and into the swamps. When those who made the swamp home saw him, they turned and ran away because they believed a ghost had come to haunt them.

A pelican then swooped in and barred his way. This peculiar bird tilted his head and looked at King Charles, then turned and walked across a wooden plank toward a rickety shack that stood under a massive canopy of moss-laden oaks and flanked by towering vines laden with that extraordinary black flower. As King Charles neared the shack, the door opened without a sound. He stood and stared at what now looked like a gaping maw. Whether he would enter was never in question; he just needed time to prepare himself.

At last, his innate curiosity was replaced by wonder of what the unknown had prepared for him. He crossed the threshold and was immediately overwhelmed by the illogical enormity of the interior.

Before him, above him, and to both sides, the shack stretched out endlessly. Vertigo set in, and as King Charles reached out in a frantic attempt to steady himself, he felt something brush against him. He recoiled from the touch but could do nothing to shield himself from the voice from his dream that said, "Fear not, He can be with you."

"Who are you? What do you want with me?" cried out King Charles. "What do you mean, 'He' can be with me? Who is this 'He' you speak of?"

"I am unimportant. I am merely His messenger. His desire is for you to lay down everything you have."

"Why should I? I'm doing just fine, thank you," he replied.

"You have a most powerful gift of persuasion that was meant to sway people to the one true God. The powers you profess to serve know this all too well. They are quite real, but they are quite false. They want nothing more than for the blood of those who follow you to be on your hands and for you to be in everlasting perdition."

"What of it? They mean nothing," said a still-defiant King Charles.

Adon Caddo responded, with dire consequence in his voice, "Do you not know, do you not understand, that whoever sheds man's blood, by man shall their own blood be shed?"[11]

King Charles was quick to his own defense, saying, "I have never shed the blood of any human."

"Yes, yes, you have, through those you employ. You are as guilty as they, and unless you repent, you shall certainly be lost for all eternity."

This statement cut King Charles to the quick. He had never been addressed in such a manner. He physically recoiled as the truth of it hit him deeply.

Adon Caddo did not give him a chance to recover but continued, "Do you not know, do you not comprehend that in the image of God has God made you and all of mankind?"[12]

King Charles suddenly felt a scorching hot wind rush against him from all directions. He looked down and realized he now stood on a precipice that, were he to take one step, he would plummet into a roiling sea of fire. Vertigo once again struck him, and as he began to fall forward, he felt Adon Caddo's hand grasp his shoulder. "It is your choice, Charles. I will release you if that is your desire, or I will keep you from the fall. Decide now: This is your only chance. Realize this: If you choose to serve God, you must relinquish everything and serve Him only."

At this moment, Charles then only heard the shrieks of those he had slaughtered. They were not in the lake of fire; they themselves were the lake of fire! The horror of it caused Charles to realize that he had only thought of the people he had affected as means to an end. They had not been of any value to him other than what he could bilk out of them. They had been nothings, meaningless and lifeless entities. But now, the reality of who he was and what he had done struck him down low to his knees. He submissively knelt on the floor and could only reach out with one bony arm to plead his cause ... absolution and forgiveness.

"How can I be free from this burden of sin, guilt, and shame? How could He ever forgive such a one as I? How?" cried Charles.

"Though your sins be as scarlet, you can be washed white as snow,"[13] said Adon Caddo. "You know who He is. He is Jesus, the Son of God. Only through Him can you be forgiven. Only by Him can you be free. Decide: Who do you serve?"

Charles, unlike the many who had been brought to this precise moment of decision, did not allow pride to take control. "I choose to serve Jesus. He is all I have truly ever desired, though I never realized it."

Suddenly, all sound ceased. All heat was vanquished. Every cry of agony ceased. He was alone, and yet he knew that he really was not. He rose, and as he stretched that long, lanky body, he felt the weight of the chains that had bound him loosen. Before him, a door opened, and the sunlight that poured through dazzled him. Charles emerged from that tiny shack, swathed in only his white sheet, totally changed.

"What must I do now?" he asked.

Adon Caddo said, "Come into the water, submerge yourself as if you have been buried, and then rise into your new life."

Charles did as he was told. He stepped into that red water and flung himself back until he was totally submerged. When he rose, he heard that voice one more time saying, "Now go. As has been done for you, do so for others, in His name only. In His name alone."

Charles walked away slowly, considering all he had gone through. He paid no attention to where his feet led him. Those who saw him only stared at this quite peculiar vision: a very tall, very thin albino man wrapped in white. As he neared the city, he saw what had been his old stage, that rickety platform built over the Mississippi. Many people saw him mount the platform, where he stood with one arm raised and his bony index finger pointed heavenward. As the days passed, Charles never moved. Many who knew him came to stare and taunt him, with no results. No one understood this new manifestation of King Charles; they were all terrified of what they saw.

At night, the vision became even more disturbing: There he stood, arm raised high toward heaven. This bizarre vision of Charles was made even more so by thousands of fireflies that illuminated him. Crowds quickly developed along the shore to gawk and ridicule him because they no longer feared him. They felt betrayed, used, and abandoned, and they began to seethe in anger. Charles then lowered his arm and pointed directly at the crowd. His voice boomed above the noise, saying, "My life was craven! It was depraved! I laid it down and abandoned it."

The crowd was stunned into silence. They had never heard King Charles speak in such a manner.

Just as they regained a sense of composure, Charles roared again, "It has been revealed to me that when you are free of your sin, you will then be truly free!"

The crowd began to howl with laughter, and then they rebelled. Many hurled mud and stones at him, but all seemed to be deflected, nothing touched him. In rage, many rushed the platform and began to shake it violently, loosening it from its moorings. Charles never moved but stood there as still as stone.

The platform began to float on the water; it floated, however, against the current. The crowds stood there and stared in wonder and amazement. Charles turned into the direction he now traveled. He was never seen in New Orleans again.

His journey took him upriver when, through no effort on his part, the platform became moored at a bend in the river, very close to the city of the red stick, Baton Rouge. The people who saw this strange visage were not antagonistic to him. They let him be; they had seen their share of lunatics in the past, and he was no exception.

Every so often, someone would be seen going up to Charles, who by now was simply known as "that crazy Preacherman." He would be seen in serious discussion with that person, who would then be led by Charles into that muddy water, where they would be baptized.

Years passed, generations came and went, but that crazy Preacherman never left his mooring. By now, no one knew where he came from, no one knew how he survived, and no one knew how his robe remained spotless white: All of this just increased his mystery.

Then one day, he was just gone. Some people said that he had fallen off the platform and drowned. Others believed that he had become a gator's meal. Others were positive that a strong, high tide had washed him away, while yet others swore that on nights when the moon was particularly full, he could be seen as he walked along the shores, bony arm held aloft toward heaven and illuminated by the light of countless fireflies, singing, "Haz you been baptized? Come wadin' in de waters wit' me!"

And then, just as mysteriously, he would be gone.

CHAPTER 9

THE ARTIST

He considered himself to be an artist of exceptional style and uncanny creative ability. And why shouldn't he? His work had garnered international attention, as evidenced by the numerous critiques, reviews, commentaries, and featured articles that had been written about him. As with many of the greats whom he considered near equals to himself (Van Gogh, Raphael, Seurat, Modigliani, and of course, Monet), his work ended abruptly. Unlike those whose accomplishments are still highly valued and cherished, however, his work has largely been forgotten, relegated to the pile of curious oddity. Perhaps on some plane of spiritual existence, he might be aware of this. If he were still among the living, he most certainly would not be pleased. He had been a huge narcissist, after all.

In his youth, he was a child alone, precocious and headstrong, but he was never lonely. The other children who could have befriended him found him to be strange and out of sorts with their childish passions. This did not bother him in the least since he found them quite inferior; therefore, he felt it his duty to look down on them.

His mother attempted to assuage what she felt was his loneliness by taking him to church, where he could meet children his own age and, of most importance, meet the One who could save his soul. He went but resented every moment. He hardened his heart, and as he grew, it was locked in a metaphorical iron box of his own creation.

When he was seven years old, he heard his own peculiar muse's call, and he responded immediately. His favorite medium was little creatures he could find around his home, such as chameleons, tiny rodents, dragonflies, and the like. As he grew older, his attention shifted to little animals such as kittens, puppies, and birds. While he did gain a modicum of satisfaction from such models, it wasn't until he focused his insatiable curiosity upon human anatomy that he found true contentment. He was particularly drawn to the voluptuous images of the Italian Renaissance and the kaleidoscopic sea of colors and nationalities that was New Orleans. He had little trouble in finding subjects that inspired him.

His first *cause célèbre*, inspired by a local Italian of the Cruti family, elicited only a tiny mention in *The Times-Picayune*. It was, however, placed on the front page, and that excited him beyond measure. He cut it out and nailed it to his wall. He had arrived! It was now only a matter of time before the whole world took notice and proclaimed that a new artistic genius had emerged, the first to do so from that cornucopia of wanton pleasures and vice, New Orleans.

Truth be told, even though *The Times-Picayune* had mentioned him, he was not that pleased with his work. He felt that it lacked finesse and that it was just a tad too heavy-handed, but nevertheless, he was most encouraged. As a self-trained artist, he took note and vowed he would learn and improve from this first endeavor. Every few months thereafter, he received more press, each article longer and more descriptive than the previous ones.

Highly encouraged, he threw himself even more enthusiastically into his work. He continued to experiment until he achieved what he considered to be his first true masterpiece: a mother and child that he named *Cortiminglia*, after the model's last name.

Following the voluminous amount of press coverage that followed the *Cortiminglia*, he decided that something very new and quite extraordinary should take place. He reasoned that, since New Orleans had long been famed as the birthplace of jazz, perhaps if he utilized that unique feature from such a wondrous city, he would receive what he so desired: immortality.

He took pen to hand and wrote a letter to the media that outlined his outrageous scheme: to wit, he would cease his work until he had been thoroughly and artistically inspired and rejuvenated. The only way this could happen was for every business and every family throughout New Orleans to have a jazz band play for the duration of the night of March 13, 1919. Much to his delight, the letter was published. Now, it was just a matter of time to see how the city would respond.

New Orleans did not disappoint. On that fateful night, from every open door and window, Euterpe's influence erupted, as the sound of jazz flooded the streets. The city, more alive than it had ever been, induced a state of euphoric giddiness in him that he had never before experienced.

As one might enjoy a seven-course gourmet feast, he relished this blissful state of joy for months. When he finally returned to work, rejuvenated and inspired, he firmly expected the press to revel in his new accomplishments. This, however, was not the case. The press hardly commented on his next two works, other than a veiled reference made to his technique which, they felt, resembled that of someone who wielded an axe. Imagine: They had the nerve to insult this paragon of artistic genius by calling him the Axeman!

To add insult to injury, something else occurred which caused him to reel with anger and confusion. A usurper, one Joseph Mumfre (a former resident of New Orleans), had moved to the City of Angels, two thousand miles away, and took credit for everything that had transpired in New Orleans, including the *Cortiminglia*.

Infuriated, enraged, and depressed, he took to the bottle, something he rarely did, as he felt it dulled his senses. As he drank, he wandered the labyrinthine streets for hours until, under the light of a full moon, he ended up far out of the city limits and in the swampy bayous.

Exhausted and depressed, he sat down on an ancient, rickety pier and let his feet dangle in the red water. A pelican swooped down and sat beside him. Try as he might, he could not rid himself of this avian intruder. Even when he stumbled to his feet to kick the intruder away, the pelican remained just slightly out of reach.

Before he became thoroughly frustrated, he heard something out in the swamp that quite amazed him: the sound of applause. Further, he noticed that the pelican had begun to waddle toward the sound. With nothing but time on his hands, he decided to follow it.

As he walked, the tendrils of an intoxicating aroma reached out and took hold of him. A hedge of vines and dark blossoms then began to entwine about his shoulders and waist and, what totally confounded him, actually moved alongside of him. He was led toward an abandoned, vine-covered shack.

As he stood and stared at the black door, he again heard the sound of applause. The door slowly opened to him, and the vines thrust him through the threshold.

He was in a long hallway; its walls were bathed in blood. Gilded frames lined the walls; in each were replicas of his handiwork. Something strange, though, they never seemed to be quite in focus but writhed like heat waves rising off a hot surface. As he was slowly propelled down the hallway, the images he had created reached out to him; their nails clawed at his flesh and began to tear him to shreds. Their screams were like daggers that tore through him.

The artist could not shield himself from the wrath that was hurled at him. A light then began to shine farther down the hallway; he ran to it but halted abruptly, as a chasm opened beneath him. A hand protruded out of the light and he heard a voice say, "Though your sins be as scarlet …"[14]

The last word the artist ever spoke was "Never!" The Artist plummeted into the depths of the bottomless chasm and was never seen or heard of again.

CHAPTER 10

WILLIE LEE

His name was Willie Lee, not William, as everyone wanted to call him and identification cards always got incorrect, not Will, because he hated abbreviations, and never, God forbid, Bill or Billy. He was either Mr. Lee or Willie, short and sweet.

Willie was a self-made man. Born to dirt-poor Baptist country folk in Pineville, Louisiana, he was raised with knowledge of the Lord. Even as a youngster, though, he did not pay much attention to all those stories of sin and redemption. They were stories that he could not touch physically; they seemed to be stories that bordered on fairy tales. If not concrete fact that he could prove, he turned away.

Willie dreamed of being a doctor, but it was the Depression, and finances were so bad. Willie vowed that, whatever it took, he would escape the snare of poverty. With that as his modus operandi, he became an obsessed overachiever in everything that came his way. He had no time for the things of God, which his parents had tried so hard to instill in him.

He was always a top student, and he excelled in sports (archery, in particular). When he was ready to go to the university (LSU, of course; was there any other?), he had to settle for a chemical engineering degree rather than a medical degree (far too expensive.) As it turned out, this decision was quicker and faster, and with the big boom of the new oil industry along the coast, well, with his brains and tenacity, he was sure to do well.

Upon graduation, he did better than well; he did great. He was immediately picked up by one of the leading petroleum companies and put to work in the field. Within a few years, he had risen to prominence. During this time, he realized that his true talent was in chemical waste management and analysis, its environmental hazards, and most importantly, how waste products could be disguised so as to not diminish corporate profits.

On his numerous outings in the field, Willie began to notice that the wildlife around the refineries appeared to suffer. Further, the land itself, once so lush, had begun to turn brown, and the water, so vital to that particular environment, had quickly turned to a toxic mix of chemical waste.

Willie then began to notice that the local Cajun population had thinned out since he started to work. He did not fully comprehend what had begun to happen until, on one of his fact-finding missions, several families approached him. They complained that the water was killing their children. Willie ignored them until the complaints became threats.

Willie was now at the threshold of a crisis of conscience, though he did not realize it. This crisis would not manifest quite yet. He realized that all of his acumen would be required so that the company would continue its business without interruption and, ergo, loss of profit.

Willie brought these problems to the attention of the corporate powers. They were unimpressed with his findings. They were, however, most definitely impressed with the implications. Rather than offer suggestions on how to proceed, they informed Willie that since he had discovered the situation and that his name was on all the findings, it was his responsibility, and his alone, to handle what could be a publicity crisis. He must now, rather than do the work he was trained for, focus his attention on how to divert all attention away from the company. If word got out that they were responsible for any environmental hazards, it would be Willie's head that would roll.

Willie returned to the field, those thick bayous Louisiana was famous for, in the hope for some kind of inspiration to guide him. On this journey, he carried many technical devices that would further determine the extent of the damage. As he wandered, he came to an area of the bayou where the swamp water was blood red, a condition he had never before encountered. As he bent over to take a few vials of the repellant water, a pelican waddled up to his side and looked at him with an avian, quizzical stare.

Willie tried to shoo the inquisitive bird away, but the pelican would have nothing to do with it. Willie decided to change his location, but as he began to walk away, the pelican blocked his path. This was repeated several times. At first, Willie thought this to be some rite of territorial defense. He then realized that the pelican was actually herding him toward an ancient wooden walkway that extended over the red water and to an island.

Ever inquisitive, Willie decided to go to the island. When he arrived, the first thing he noticed was a very strange shack that seemed to defy logic. As he walked closer, he began to notice an aroma that was nothing short of intoxicating. As he breathed deep, he became more and more relaxed and at ease. For someone who was usually wound up in a knot of raw energy, this was a pleasant sensation, and one he chose to savor.

As he inspected the island, his attention was arrested by how magnificent the giant moss-laden oaks were and how strongly exquisite the vines of black blossoms seemed to be. As he stooped to pluck one, the door of the shack soundlessly opened. It seemed to beckon to him to enter. Once again, his curiosity got the best of him; he walked in.

What he beheld took his breath away. It was the bayou in its original primordial splendor, not what it had become. As he continued to wander, he was spellbound by the outrageous abundance of wildlife, the lushness of the vegetation, the glorious miasma of wild and wonderful fragrances, and finally, the original inhabitants who lived in a paradise unspoiled by corporate pollution and greed.

Willie was so overcome that his knees gave out. He sat down on the moist earth and just took it all in.

"His work is marvelous, is it not?" came a voice, but from where, Willie had no idea.

"Who's there?" he asked. "What do you mean?"

"You know precisely Who I mean, though you've tried to ignore Him all of your life."

Willie was taken aback, and even slightly irked, by this sudden intrusion. He responded, "If you're talking about some God … out there, I don't believe in a God. I believe in facts, hard data, something real, nothing ethereal or make-believe."

"Do you not know, do you not realize, that which may be known of God has been manifest to all men, including you, since time began? His work, His creation of the universe, is clearly seen by everyone, so that no one is without excuse.[15]

"A denial of God has gone on since the dawn of time. They knew God but did not glorify Him. Nor were they grateful. They became vain in their imaginations, and their foolish, foolish hearts were darkened,[16] like yours may soon become."

Willie had begun to feel a pang in his heart: why, or from what, he did not know.

The voice continued, "Man thinks himself wise, but he is a fool to deny the Creator. Man has changed the glory of the incorruptible God into an image made like to corruptible man!"[17]

"I have done no such thing," protested Willie.

"But you have; you are, even now. You are so close, so very close to exchanging the truth of God for the lies of man. Be warned: God will give you up to a reprobate mind filled with all unrighteousness. Know this: You will suffer the consequences of your decision. You are on a precipice; it is your decision that will determine your everlasting future, not His."

At that moment, the interior of the shack, that beautiful re-creation of the bayou, suddenly turned into a fiery, roiling mass inhabited by a multitude of anguished people. The deafening sound they made was composed of every discordant, anguished cry imaginable. As they frantically tried to crawl out, they would just miss the edge that would have given them that chance. The mass would then roil and churn, and they would all be swept away to be replaced by even more tormented souls.

"Make it stop! Make it all go away! Of all the demons sent to torment me, why do you torment me so?" cried Willie.

"I am no demon, of that you can be sure," said Adon Caddo. "By your acknowledgment that demons exist, you are mightily aware God Himself exists. You are without excuse! You must admit Him into your heart or be lost for all eternity."

With that declaration, Willie gasped as he saw himself, tormented nearly beyond recognition, emerge from that roiling mass, a writhing human anguished beyond description. Willie screamed a scream so deep, so primitive, that the entire vision exploded and vanished.

Willie was now alone in the moonlight, as countless fireflies provided further, magical illumination. Even more peculiar, that bizarre pelican stood before him, cocked his head, and flapped his wings, and then he made a guttural sound that Willie forevermore believed was that blasted bird's attempt at laughter.

Willie, exhausted from his experience, fell asleep under those massive oaks, soothed to sleep by the intoxicating aroma of the black gardenias. He awoke to a sun high up in the sky. Willie stood up, brushed himself off, and began to return to the mainland, when he heard the clarion call of the common loon. He had no idea that the loon was the harbinger of a soul that would soon confess and be illuminated by the true light from above.

Willie was faced with monumental decisions. He could ignore them and perish, or act upon them, regardless of whether he lived or died. He decided that he must make every effort to insure the continuation of the life God had created, and in that decision, he had stepped onto the way that leads unto life.[18]

CHAPTER 11
EURYNOMOUS L'ETOILE DU MATIN

No mortal ever recognized Adon Caddo's success with the transformative conversion of King Charles; however, it did not go unnoticed in the spiritual realm. As with any created being, Adon Caddo could be misled if he was not diligent with the ongoing cultivation of his love and obedience for God. He knew that his ability to love was a gift to be cherished, as it should have been for every creature, and for that he was very grateful.

As hard to grasp as it was, however, all did not accept the gift of God's love. There were those who rejected it, resented it, and even rebuked it, yet God continually offers His outstretched hand to those willing to abide on His terms. In the spiritual realm, there was no concept of redemption. Redemption had been reserved for man alone. What was done was done, faith accomplished, fait accompli ... or not. It was always the individual's choice.

One day, as Pel fished, and Adon Caddo tended to his black gardenias as he communed with God, an enormous gator swam down the bayou. On its back, with one foot lazily dangled in the water, was a body reclined as if on a chaise lounge. This stretched-out body belonged to one Eurynomous L'Etoile du Matin. Eury, as he insisted he be addressed, appeared to be one of those extraordinary Nubians whose beautiful skin was like a panther's, so intensely black that, in certain light, it had a blue cast. The lustrous tone of his flawless skin offset perfect teeth that were so astonishingly white one would think he could light up the night sky with his smile (some even confessed that they believed he smiled with excessive lavishness, but that he chewed with enviable acumen). His large sable eyes swam in glistening pools of white. His straight, slicked-back hair reflected any light that it might encounter. His attire was a simple, faded denim overall, ragged at the cuffs, with only one strap attached, as the other strap hung and exposed half of his lithely muscular chest. He was, in a word, beautiful, to the point of distraction.

Eury was definitely not a native of this particular swamp. In fact, he was quite new to the area. Once he was seen, however, he could not be forgotten.

Eury was quite bright, with a keen, quick mind that retained everything. Further, he was conversant in an endless array of languages on an inexhaustible number of subjects. He chose, however, to converse in the colloquial vernacular simply because, as he told others, he thought it felt rather nice as it rolled over his tongue and off his palate. The truth was that he enjoyed making a mockery of those he mimicked and ridiculed.

A sudden movement caught his eye: A shrub on a tiny island he passed had moved. He thumped the side of the gator with his foot, and the reptile responded and swam to the island's shore. Eury did not disembark his ride but continued to recline on the living leatherback chaise lounge.

"I knows youze dere! I'ze a-bin watchin' youze an' dat stupid penguin of yurs fur quite a tad. I kin heah youze a'breathin," Eury said in his best, but nevertheless irritating, imitation of a deep, Creole-inspired Southern accent.

"No … no, you cannot," said a voice from within the shrub. "I do not breathe, neither do you. Remember? And the bird is a pelican, not a penguin," said a very irritated Adon Caddo, who knew precisely with whom he spoke.

"Oh, yeah, Caddo, dat's raight," Eury said. "Youze en' me, we'ze wat's called 'spirit beings.' We doan need dat stuff az deeze yoomans do."

"Get to the point, Eury, then, please, kindly leave."

"Caddo, Caddo, Caddo, my boy, is dat any way ta speak ta yur ol' friend Eury?"

"Old? Yes. Friend? I think not. And Eury, if you are going to talk to me, do so without that ridiculous accent. You sound moronic."

"Caddo, you are such a bore. Has anyone ever told you that? I mean really, has anyone *ever* told you that? You are simply no fun at all; you never have been. You and the other Adons, good grief, what a matched set of unmitigated fossils you are. With everything in creation at your fingertips ... well, it's not worth the effort to make you see the truth. Took me forever to figure out where you were hiding since You Know Who kicked y'all out of heaven."

"He did not kick us out, as you know all too well. We were repositioned for His divine purpose. You, on the other hand, it was your decision and yours alone to be swayed to leave by that father of yours. You could have stayed, but oh no, you and your kind are never satisfied with anything He gives to us."

"Oh please, Caddo, to sit around kissing His feet and lapping up His every word like a cat with a bowl of milk. Makes me sick; what a waste."

"Your words, not mine."

"You were one tough Adon to find, I'll give you that. It took me ages. He is so cagey sometimes. Anyway, I was swimming one day in the Yellow River. You know the one, way over there in China. Anyway, it hit me. It's just not right for a river to have such a strong color; something was off, different. I had an idea, but I needed to check it out first. I went to Egypt and saw how green the Nile was, then to Europe and realized that the Danube was blue for a reason. Then, like a bolt out of the blue, it dawned on me: The Adons had been sent to each of the world's the great rivers. It was the Adons who were responsible for the colors of the rivers. You, you're the bloody red one. After that, it didn't take too long to track you down."

"Please, get to the point, and then leave me alone."

"You're such a killjoy! Okay, the reason I have sought you out is this: I have a message for you. I do, I really do. My father is not at all pleased with how you interfered, disrupted, and basically ruined his plans for King Charles. My father put a lot of work into him, and then you had to go and just ruin everything."

"Your father," said an exasperated Adon Caddo, "your father is a liar, the father of lies, actually.[19] Why should I care if his plan was ruined?"

"Why, Caddo, how can you say such a thing? Well, my friend, you should care, that's for sure," said Eury. "It's like this: My father is mad at you. I do not mean sophomoric mad: No, I mean full-blown, smoke from his nostrils, raging mad at you. He wants revenge. He's got something big … no, something huge … no, no, something enormous planned. It's going to damage and affect you in a very profound way that you're not going to like one teensy weensy little bit.

"I've always liked you, Caddo; never understood you, but I've always liked you. Don't ask me why, I just do. Really! Sooooooo, just because I like you, I'm here to give you a heads-up, something He won't do. You Know Who I mean. Why am I telling you this? Why am I telling you this? I'll tell you why I'm telling you this. This is why I'm telling you this: I don't want you to get caught. I want to give you and that stupid parrot a chance to get off this pathetic little island in time, in plenty of time. See, I'm your friend, I really am."

"What's that old saying? 'With friends like you, who needs enemies?' You have done your job, lackey, now do me a kindness and just be gone." Adon Caddo stormed off into the shack.

"Well, I never! Don't say you weren't warned … fool!" Eury kicked the side of the gator, and off they went.

CHAPTER 12
STORM OF STORMS

As the years passed, extraordinary experiences continued to occur as countless individuals found themselves under the influence of the Black Gardenia and its amazing, secretive inhabitant. Remarkably, time itself behaved in a nonlinear fashion within the Black Gardenia. Adon Caddo and Pel could enter it, and when they emerged, years might have passed. It is a pity that the volumes of those experiences that should have been written never were. What has been recorded is blessed little. This was due, in part, to the following event.

It began on a dull gray day, not all that unusual. The sky was not blue but a silvery brushed nickel. The Spanish moss, usually swollen with abundant humidity and far too heavy to capture a breeze, began to ever so slowly wave in a subtle wind that had begun to blow in from the Gulf.

Early in the morning, Adon Caddo, as was his custom, ventured out of the shack and went to the water's shoreline to examine what the morning had in store. Pel stood beside Adon Caddo and examined the morning from the perceptive perspective only a pelican possesses. They both noticed that the water was just a slight bit agitated, nothing out of the ordinary for an early December morning. Pel chose to examine it a bit further and flew out and about. When he returned, Adon Caddo could easily see that Pel was exhausted and had a bad go of it. Something was definitely out of the ordinary.

Just then, the sound of thunder shook the little island so violently that the Black Gardenia rose off of the ground and then resettled in a slightly different location. Pel looked at Adon Caddo as if to say, "Oh, that can't be good."

Adon Caddo and Pel walked back to the Black Gardenia. Before they got to the door, another clap of thunder crashed, followed by a lightning bolt that streaked across the sky, far too close for comfort. They heard an explosion and assumed that the lightning had struck some object, like a home or a barn, far off in the distance.

The wind continued to gather strength and was soon joined by heavy sprays of water that flew with brutal, horizontal velocity. Even this was not so out of the ordinary; many a storm that had come in from the Gulf acted in such a fashion. Adon Caddo and Pel decided to ride it out in the Black Gardenia. Just as the door began to open, an apocalyptic thunder crash exploded overhead.

Adon Caddo and Pel had no way of knowing that what headed their way was in no way typical. It was, in fact, so atypical that one could only assume it had received help from an unnatural source. One would have assumed correctly. Eury had warned of such an event.

The storm surges, combined with rising tides, battered and destroyed the extensive New Orleans levee system. As a result, unprecedented flooding devastated 80 percent of the city and nearby parishes. Thousands were left homeless, and thousands more perished.

Adon Caddo knew he must do something, but he had no idea what that something should be. As the violence of the waters increased, and the winds roared, Pel suddenly began to squawk hysterically, something he had never done before. Pel frantically swam out onto the bayou and dove into the water. When he surfaced, he began to swim ashore; Adon Caddo realized that Pel was towing something with that enormous beak. Adon Caddo rushed to the water's edge and, in horror, realized that he was towing a little child. Adon Caddo pulled the child from the roiling water as Pel, exhausted, waddled onto land and collapsed, too weak to move.

Adon Caddo then heard the frenzied cries for help from countless others who had been caught in the massive tidal surges. Adon Caddo, knowing he would be in direct violation of God's request if he were to help those desperate souls, pondered his predicament: Should he help them for all the right reasons, but disobey God's request, or should he stand firm on his island and watch as the desperate and dying pleaded for help as they passed by, to certain doom?

He did not have much time to consider his situation: He saw another child drowning in the water and, without thought, flung his wrist in the child's direction. As he did so, a vine as strong as rope flew out of his cloak and wrapped around the child's hand. Adon Caddo was thus able to pull the child to shore.

Adon Caddo realized that the child would have drowned if he had trusted his own instinct and not his faith in God. Empowered and inspired with this knowledge, Adon Caddo stood at the water's edge and created a bridge of entwined vines that spanned the width of the bayou. By doing this, Adon Caddo enabled anyone who was endangered to reach out and grab a vine, haul himself or herself up, and then walk on the bridge he had created to the shore, to safety.

It took very little time for Adon Caddo to see the bridge put to use. A young couple that had been washed away saw the bridge and took hold of it. Once they got on the island, the Black Gardenia opened its door. The couple, at first apprehensive, realized there was no other option; they entered to discover a long, dry tunnel that eventually opened onto high, dry land. Where? They had no idea, but they were now quite safe and very, very thankful.

As the wind howled, the rain poured, and the water rose to a dangerous level, Adon Caddo stood as the anchor of the bridge for the duration of the cataclysm. Countless numbers of potentially doomed people were rescued when they saw that astounding vine bridge. At first, Adon Caddo tried to keep count of the many numbers of people who owed their lives to the bridge, but as the storm increased in intensity, so too did the numbers of people in harm's way; he was unable to keep count.

It was now very late in the day. When the threat of further

damage had ceased, Adon Caddo released his grip upon the bridge. As he walked to the Black Gardenia, he saw something far off in the distance that rode the waves like a galleon. It appeared to be a giant log, but with enormous, reptilian eyes. A massive gator floated on the surface of the water, and straddled upon its back, still holding a large blue drink that was topped off by a paper umbrella and an assortment of colorful fruit slices, was someone Adon Caddo never wanted to see or hear again: Eury!

Eury, thrilled that he had finally been noticed, lifted his glass toward Adon Caddo in a sarcastic mock toast and yelled from his leather barge, "Caddo, Caddo, Caddo! Just look at your soaked little red self! Drenched to the bone, as you've furtively slaved away to hold that pathetic, deficient, puny little bridge in place. And why do you do all that? I'll tell you why: on account of a few feeble little ol' humans, who might be saved and then be completely rejected by Him. Oh, how typical. How sick. How pathetic you really are! Why, just the other day, I was talking with my father about how sick and pathetic you and your ilk really are. You do remember my father, don't you? Oh, of course you do. You two were once so close; thick as thieves, as they say. You ever wonder who 'they' is? 'They' are? Whatever. Yeah, that's it. You ever wonder who they are? Or maybe 'were'? You know, they 'are' might be 'were,' if they didn't come through the storm, so they could be 'were' and not 'are,' or even 'is.' Does it matter? It really doesn't matter who they is, was, were, or are, now, does it?

"What happened to you, Caddo, my boy? What happened? Anyway, dear Papa's favorite subject for discussion (except, perhaps, how to foil You Know Who's plans) is how pathetic, weak, sorry, pathetic (did I already say pathetic? I did, didn't I? Ah, it makes no never mind), and submissive all of you Adons really are. Really! Just listen to me; I'm rambling again, aren't I? That's a bad habit, I suppose, ramblin', I mean. I need to train myself to stop, but I'm just a ramblin' kind of guy, I s'pose. I think it could be an annoyance to someone as erudite as you. Maybe not. Maybe so. Who's to say anyway? What do you think? You do realize that you brought this storm on all by yourself. You know that, don't you? It's entirely your fault. All of it. ALL…OF…IT! All of the lives lost … your fault! All of the destruction … your fault. I told you this would happen, now, didn't I? But would you listen to me? No."

As Eury prattled on and on and on, Adon Caddo, quite unnoticed by Eury, pointed his index finger at the surface of the water. With stealth and subtlety, Adon Caddo began to make an almost imperceptible circular motion with his finger. As Eury continued with his incessant chatter, Adon Caddo continued with that circular motion and created a whirlpool that grew larger and larger.

Eury, now quite exasperated, yelled out to Adon Caddo, "Would you please stop that motion thing with your finger? You're making me seasick!"

Adon Caddo stopped and then casually pointed for Eury to look behind him. Eury turned and gasped, but before he could do anything, he was sucked off the back of the gator and into the swirling vortex of an enormous hole that gaped hungrily in the water behind him. Eury's time in this dimension had come to an abrupt (and for Adon Caddo, a blessed) end.

From his vantage point on the island, Adon Caddo was unable to comprehend the cataclysmic devastation that the hurricane had wreaked. It was not until the water levels had receded that he realized things might never be the same again. Even Pel, most dismayed after he had flown a survey around the swamp, stood by Adon Caddo and just stared. As they shook their heads in wonder, Adon Caddo and Pel went into the Black Gardenia.

Miraculously, not a bush or tree or plank of wood on the island had seen the slightest bit of damage. As time would tell, this did not go unnoticed, particularly when events of biblical proportions began.

CHAPTER 13

BEGINNINGS OF THE END

Though multitudes adamantly deny it, since Adam ushered sin into every aspect of creation, its ravages have never ceased but only continued to build momentum. One of the results was the earth's gradual geophysical deterioration, from a state of perfection to that of a lurking time bomb that awaited just the right fuse to wreak havoc and cause massive destruction.

Case in point: Far beneath the swamps and bayous where the Black Gardenia existed, there were extensive and lengthy tunnels with enormously tall salt domes. The ruling government of the time utilized these tunnels and domes as a method to house its vast energy reserves. Stored within this system of chambers were barrels of natural gas and oil, and even massive amounts of nuclear waste. The great scientific minds failed to realize, or simply chose to ignore, something quite elementary: Salt was dissolved by water. When the salt towers dissolved, massive sinkholes appeared that engulfed entire towns, and worse. To add insult to injury, natural gas seeped up through the ground and awaited only a lit match or a strike of lightning to be ignited.

That ignition finally, and quite suddenly, came after the great vanishing of all believers occurred. A worldwide phenomenon, their disappearance was the catalyst that launched the world into innumerable cataclysms, famines, disease, and wars. Nothing like it had ever occurred, and within seven years, the earth had become a vast, violent, and viral wasteland. Even then, the pierced hands of Jesus were continually held out to anyone who would simply believe that He had died and risen to life, just for them. Yet the multitudes that survived continued to curse God even more vehemently.

Adon Caddo had been shielded from this while inside the Black Gardenia. Time, always off-kilter within the Black Gardenia, did not travel in the accepted linear fashion, as normal terrestrials were accustomed to. No, time could travel anywhere it wanted to once inside the Black Gardenia. As such, Adon Caddo was totally unaware of the crisis the world faced, until the day the island was shook so violently that those ancient, giant oaks actually lost several massive branches and crashed to the ground. This was followed by a stench so vile that even a creature such as Adon Caddo noticed it, as did Pel, who passed out, seriously affected. Adon Caddo picked him up, cradled him in his arms, and nursed him back to health.

As Adon Caddo surveyed the destruction, he saw a world he no longer recognized. The dense foliage around the swamp had been decimated, as far as the eye could see. The water, now brackish and vile, showed no sign of life. The only thing untouched had been the shack, the walkway, the protective vines, and those amazing black gardenias. Instinctively, Adon Caddo plucked several blossoms, crushed them in his hands, and scattered them upon the waters as a worshipful offering to God. The waters began to churn and surge, and wherever a portion of a blossom made contact with the surface of the water, a noticeable change occurred. The water became transparent and quite blue. If tasted, the water was now sweet. In what had become a vast wasteland, the Black Gardenia was an oasis.

Now fully recovered, Pel wandered to the water's edge; he took a cautionary look around and then jumped in. He made an inspection of the island from his watery vantage point and then flew above and around the island. When he had completed his surveillance, he returned to Adon Caddo's side, looked up at him, and squawked approval. In the time it took for him to complete his surveillance, the island had become encircled by blue, clear water and was now an open invitation to any who might have survived the catastrophe.

Later in the day, a lone straggler was seen as he staggered down what had been an old dirt road. His clothing, dust covered and torn, hung from his emaciated shoulders. His eyes were hollow orbs that had witnessed far too much pain and misery. He had open sores on his face and hands. In the distance, he saw a pile of rocks (boulders, actually).

He suddenly dashed to the rocks, and when he was upon them, his anguish could be heard as pleaded, "I've run to you rocks to hide my face."

To his astonishment, the rocks themselves suddenly cried out, "Be gone! We are not your hiding place."

The rocks abruptly scattered and left him exposed and bare. They would not, could not, be participants in whatever prompted his anguish.

The man, totally defeated, turned and staggered to the water's edge. Pel noticed him, flew out to the edge of the island to the walkway, and squawked. The man saw Pel, turned, and walked across the walkway, then he fell at water's edge and began to drink. When he had somewhat recovered, he sat up. Pel sat beside him and cocked his head, as if to say, "What happened?"

Head in hands, the man began to convulse; he said, with anguished tears, "Gone. All gone. Everyone I ever loved, everything I ever cared about ... gone. What am I going to do? Where can I go? Everything gone, everything ruined."

Pel looked at him as if he understood every word. He probably did: Pel had become, after all, an ageless avian, wise beyond his years, through his association with Adon Caddo at the Black Gardenia.

Pel rested his beak on the man's thigh and listened as he continued, "What kind of God would do this? What kind of monster would delight in the misery He has wrought? I want no part of this God!"

At the same time, Adon Caddo extended a tendril vine with a single bud and slowly, empathetically, caressed the man's shoulder. Rather than recoil, the man melted at the touch. The bud slowly opened to reveal a beautiful black gardenia that released its subtle fragrance. The man, oblivious and unaware of the blossom, simply inhaled.

The effect of the blossom relaxed the man and penetrated his soul to such a degree that he could actually hear the subtle voice of Adon Caddo, saying, "For God so loved the world that He ..."[20]

Before Adon Caddo could finish, the man sat bolt upright and shouted, "Stop it! Just ... stop it! That is all a lie. What kind of love would do this? I want no part of it!" The man stood up and ran to the water, which now boiled red as blood. He threw himself in and was no more. The water returned to its blue, passive state.

Adon Caddo pondered this. What he could never understand, never fathom, after the eons that he had witnessed, was why anyone would choose to turn away from the free gift of eternal life. Over and over and over, like music in your head that plays and plays, he saw it happen, time and time again.

More stragglers began to pass the island. Many just went on by, as if they listened to a voice that intentionally enticed them away from what could be their only salvation. Others, as if in a trance, found their way to the water but were unable to comprehend its significance.

Adon Caddo could hear their cries as they passed by. He marveled at the diversity of their complaints against God. For instance:

"I am a scientist. I believe only in concrete facts that I can hear, see, or touch. There is no God if I cannot touch and feel that reality. There is no proof."

Adon Caddo had heard that one millions of times. He knew from his long observance of the human race that if they admitted that there was a God, they must then be accountable to Him. This was something their pride and arrogance simply could not allow.

"How can there be a God when everyone knows we are a product of evolution, of natural selection? There is no God."

If it weren't so tragic to hear people wail on and on about this, Adon Caddo would have found that those arguments bordered on the ridiculous. He knew that if humans truly believed such tripe, then they would believe they were not answerable for their actions and therefore immune to God's judgment.

"God is love? Oh please, what a travesty. If God is love, why has all of this happened? What kind of love is that?"

Adon Caddo knew and never questioned that God was, is, and always will be love. He did not understand why God put him in certain situations, but that did not negate God's love for him. Adon Caddo knew that the absence of love was sin, and that absence was rebellion against God. Further, that absence was the ultimate cause of all suffering, the cause of spiritual and physical death, and the source of misery and sickness.

But there were those amongst the throng whose spirits had not yet closed and who were able to realize that they still might be saved from further destruction and devastation. For them, they began to hear a voice far off in the distance, a voice that had not been heard in this region for years upon years. The voice, though ancient with age, had the strength of a voice in its prime.

"Haz you been baptized? Haz you been baptized?" That old Preacherman, at one time known as King Charles the Voodoo King, attired in his white sheet, suddenly appeared around a bend of the bayou of that forsaken swamp. He stood on what was left of his wooden raft and propelled it by the use of a long, gnarled limb that he plunged to the water's depth and then pushed.

Pel flew out to meet him and sat at the front of the raft, where he became quite regal as the figurehead of this most unconventional craft. The Preacherman docked his raft by the island side of the walkway and, rather than stand on land, walked immediately into the water and, the limb now grasped in both his ancient hands, raised his bone-thin arms into the air and said, with power and authority, "Come, chil'ren; come, chil'ren; come wadin' in de waters wit' me."

Cries rose up from those by the water's edge: "But the water! God's gonna trouble the water."

"Yes, chil'ren, yes. God's gonna trouble the water! For YOU He is gonna trouble de waters."

Adon Caddo, as God's representative, knew that this was his cue. He extended a viney, blossom-covered arm into the water. The water immediately began to churn and gurgle.

"Praise God, praise God!" a jubilant Preacherman sang out. "Come, chil'ren, come! Now's da time! Repent your sins! Confess Jesus as your savior! Dis is da lass chance ya eva' gonna get. Not a moment t' lose, not a moment. He's a-comin'! He's a-comin'!"

One by one, they came to the Preacherman, and one by one, they confessed and were then submerged. When they were raised from the water, they each had a visible glow that shone about them. As the last one rose from the water, the sound of a tremendous trumpet burst through the air. Those who had been baptized were suddenly caught up into the air.

At the same moment, Adon Caddo, with Pel firmly holding onto his shoulder, was suddenly transported into the heavenly realm, where they found themselves mounted upon a great white stallion. He was joined by all of the Adons and their unique companions. Each Adon rode upon their own great white steed. They galloped majestically behind the King of Kings, their beloved Adonai, the Lord of Lords. His eyes were on fire, and he wore upon His head many crowns. His blood-stained garment transformed into a blazing white as He glowed against the sky. He was followed by each of the now-blazing Adons, their inherent colors streaming behind them like banners in this glorious celestial display. Each Adon had, at long last, been reunited with their King whom they adored, and they rode with Him as He dealt with the final terrestrial matters.

CHAPTER 14
FOREVER AND FOREVER

When His work had finally been completed, and the last soul had entered the celestial city, the golden threads of the stairs simply vanished. The redeemed multitudes of multitudes joined in with the full angelic host to praise the Most High God. Since time itself had ceased, the duration of their praise was irrelevant.

At some point during this celebration, God Himself erased all memory of their terrestrial existence, so that they would never be eternally burdened by the memories of those who were lost. They were now truly and totally free from death, from sorrow, and from all pain. They would no longer have the need for tears because the former things had passed away, and all things had now become, and would remain so always, new.

The Adons were finally, joyfully, and forever reunited, and they freely rejoiced. Their reunion was both jubilant and poignant, as they rushed to each other with wild abandon and embraced.

The first to see Adon Caddo was Adon Huangse, from the land of the Far East. Adon Huangse had been stationed at the great river that his presence turned a golden yellow. During his tenure, he witnessed and influenced the rise and fall of countless kingdoms and cultures. It was Adon Huangse who followed this portion of humanity in its dispersion from Babel. It was Adon Huangse who subtly influenced the development of a common tongue comprised of pictographs that were based upon the Word. It had been a difficult challenge, but once the precedent of the Word hidden in plain sight within the language had been established, the results were as golden as his river.

The next to greet Adon Caddo were the Adon Irtiu and Adon Shesep. Both bore the responsibility to influence the Kemet people: Adon Irtiu had been assigned the White Nile, and Adon Shesep the Blue. Though they had never been in contact with each other, their respective luminosities attempted to influence that great civilization along the river that flowed through the Upper and Lower Kingdoms. Their success was negligible, in that they only swayed the heart of one ruler, who was then declared a heretic. Yet, this king's words echoed throughout recorded time in praise of the singular God. "O sole God," this king had said, "like whom there is no other. Thou didst create the world according to thy desire whilst thou wert alone. Thou settest every man in his place. Thou art the lord of them all!"[21]

Other than that one defining moment, this people, with multiple and miraculous opportunities, rejected the one true God in favor of a plethora of demonic deities, who held them captive for millennia.

Adon Blauen followed the Adons Irtiu and Shesep. His dazzling blue river that flowed through the continent of Europe had shaped generation after generation of humanity's most gifted musicians and, in numerous ways, had led multitudes to the truth.

Then there was the Adon Topaaz who, eons ago, allowed his feet to touch the water of the great subcontinent's major waterway, which then turned it into a pinkish hue. As a result, he was instantly mistaken and worshipped as a great god. Of course, he would never accept such misdirected adulation, but nothing he did would assuage the humans. To finally be released from such a burden brought a song to his heart.

Adon Igalaurak had been assigned to the farthest reaches of the north and resided unseen, but certainly not unnoticed, by those known as the Inuit. It was they who devised his name, Igalaurak, because he was as clear as the purest ice. They knew he was there amongst them, but they rarely saw even his silhouette, let alone his full image. His clarity, however, always prompted them to be as truthfully clear as he was.

Adon Negro Aguas had found himself perched atop the Nevado Mismi region of the Andes Mountains. Those who had been entrusted to his influence, a very superstitious and spiritually inclined people, knew of his presence, though they would never venture into his realm. Adon Negro Aguas had been very successful in preparing their hearts for the arrival of the Caucasians, who brought knowledge of the one true God, though their methods of conversion left multitudes disillusioned and disenfranchised.

Adon Halkidon was the only Adon responsible for two rivers, these being the Tigris and the Euphrates. He dwelt, isolated, between the two parallel river courses. Though the people of this region were generally tolerant of those with opposing views, they favored hostility toward those who professed belief in the one true God. This was a great burden to Adon Halkidon.

From the Land Down Under came Adon Tongala, whose extreme efforts to persuade the aboriginal population to turn their sights upon God proved a dismal failure. As with other cultures the Adons had encountered, the hearts of native populations, with very few and rare exceptions, were locked upon fraudulent deities they believed inhabited every aspect of nature. Absurd, of course, but when a heart is locked, it is impossible for it to be unlocked without the true God, Who alone has the key.

The rivers of the final two Adons were the Pishon and the Gishon, but both had long since vanished. One might think that this would leave these two Adons with plenty of time on their hands. Not so! The opposite, in fact, was true. Because they had no responsibility for a single region, they were free to travel wherever the Spirit directed them. In this fashion, they were able to affect and direct far more lives than had they remained stationary. So, as with their brother Adons, they inconspicuously influenced the affairs of man and waited for the day they would finally return home. Now that it had arrived, their joy was euphoric and contagious.

After their eons of separation had finally ended, the Adons instinctively formed a circle and majestically extended their wings, which then united the tips. As they further extended their wings, they walked backwards, which increased the size of the circle. As the circle expanded, the Adons began to slowly rise higher and higher. As they rose, they glowed brighter and brighter, until their combined emanations of multicolored light intermingled and became dazzlingly white.

The Adons rejoiced with the legions of angels and the vast multitudes of the redeemed. As they did so, the Adons suddenly found themselves seated upon a great pearl, high atop their new vantage point above the gates of the great city. Three Adons sat above each of the four walls.

The Adons were home at last, and as is universally known, there is simply no place like it. Though he would never, could never admit it, Adon Caddo suspected that his seat glowed with just a touch more hued intensity than did the others. After all, he was red, for goodness sake.

EPILOGUE

If you are a being whose age means nothing, and who has far more important things to do than write, it is doubtful that the plethora of experiences you endured would be recorded for those who might find them of interest. Therefore, the discovery of the preceding tales is all the more amazing. Where they came from is as mysterious as both the Black Gardenia itself and its extraordinary occupant.

Who knows? Perhaps there are tales from the other Adons that may one day turn up. As a matter of fact, there have been some very peculiar and promising rumors of a discovery along the Huang He River in China.

One can only hope.

ENDNOTES

1. Matthew 25:40
2. Revelation 22:13
3. 1 Thessalonians 1:4
4. 1 John 4:1–6
5. Proverbs 4:18
6. Esther 4:14
7. Revelation 22:2
8. Isaiah 30:21
9. Revelation 3:20
10. Philippians 2:12
11. Genesis 9:6
12. Genesis 1:27
13. Isaiah 1:18
14. Isaiah 1:18
15. Romans 1:20
16. Romans 1:20
17. Romans 1:23
18. Matthew 7:14
19. John 8:44
20. John 3:16
21. "Great Hymn to Aten," taken from *Tutankhamen: Amenism, Atenism and Egyptian Monotheism*, by E. A. W. Budge, 1923, copyright not renewed.